Careless Talk

Careless Talk

JAMES FRIEL

MACMILLAN LONDON LIMITED

First published 1992 by
MACMILLAN LONDON LIMITED
a division of Pan Macmillan Publishers Limited
Cavaye Place London SW10 9PG
and Basingstoke

Associated companies in Auckland, Budapest, Dublin, Gaborone,
Harare, Hong Kong, Kampala, Kuala Lumpur, Lagos, Madras, Manzini,
Melbourne, Mexico City, Nairobi, New York, Singapore, Sydney,
Tokyo and Windhoek

ISBN 0–333–574346

A CIP catalogue record for this book is available from
the British Library

Phototypeset by Intype, London
Printed by Billing & Sons Ltd, Worcester

Acknowledgements

The author and publishers would like to express their gratitude to the following who have very kindly given their permission for the use of copyright materials:

Penguin Books for permission to quote from *Speaking Of Siva* by Basavanna, translated by A K Ramanujan (Penguin Classics, 1973), copyright © A K Ramanujan, 1973.

Chatto & Windus for permission to quote from *Confession Of A Murderer* by Joseph Roth.

Faber & Faber for permission to quote from the *Four Quartets* by T.S. Eliot.

Every effort has been made to trace all copyright holders but if any has been inadvertently overlooked, the author and publishers will be pleased to make the necessary arrangement at the first opportunity.

Our imagination is always stronger than our conscience.
JOSEPH ROTH

'Come, come,' cried Emma, feeling this to be an unsafe subject. 'I must beg you not to talk of the sea. It makes me envious and miserable – I who have never seen it.'
JANE AUSTEN

History is now and England.
T. S. ELIOT

Look, the world, in a swell
Of waves, is beating on my face.
BASAVANNA

I've had long years to mull this tale over in my mind and I'm still disgusted that it's me who's forced to tell it. By rights there should be folk queuing up to tell it for me but I can no longer afford to wait while the world catches up.

Call me impatient if you like. I've been called worse.

You see, I've read every war book in Sandown library and nowhere am I mentioned except in passing and my name not even given. I call it criminal to so neglect an historical figure which is what I am though still living.

This tale is my way of getting the attention I deserve.

1

Mother loved dying. It was something she did well. It was something she did often. She'd lie back on the sofa in our front parlour in Cheamish, west of Chester, and die. '

Plump but exquisite she was with her auburn hair tumbling loose and her purple wraparound undone, moaning softly at me like the sea as heard in a shell.

'I'm going, Belle, I'm going, I'm all but gone. I'm floating. I'm fading. I'm fading clean away.'

Her voice would be no more than a sigh and her eyes they'd flutter in a manner suggestive of a soul departing.

At times I'd have sworn I'd seen her spirit rise up and travel to the very rim of life itself where it might well have dropped from sight had I not been there to call it back.

I was no bigger than a whisper but I had my part to play. Mother was my all-in-all and I'd cry out, 'Mother, don't go, don't leave me! Mother! Mother!'

I was not as you see without dramatic skill myself.

I knew it was just fiddle-diddle the lot of it but did I care? You had to be sincere or where was the fun? Mother insisted I mourn as if for real. Only misery at its heaviest could tether her soul to this sad earth.

'Cry harder, our Mabel, or I'll float off and leave you for good. Then where will you be?'

I look back and I think Happy Times for death was a game we both enjoyed. It filled up the empty days of which we were never short in Cheamish. In winter we'd play it with the dark outside and the lamps on low. In summer there'd be a breeze through the open windows looking set to waft Mother heavenwards. The tops of the lilies would look in and nod as if in approval.

The game done, death denied and love triumphant, we'd settle back with me at Mother's feet and feeling guilty for some times there'd be when I'd not cried and Mother would be angry.

'There must always be tears of some description. It'd not be right to watch a person pass on with dry eyes.'

Her own eyes would be as hard as toffee but she'd relent in a moment. Such softness she had about her. She'd pull me to her like I was a belt and hug and fuss me only to leave go of a sudden and with no warning as if she'd forgotten I was even there.

I take it such a memory occurs in the Great War with me no less than four and no more than eight. I say this for I've no sense of Father thereabouts and only the vaguest of Miss Bird who lived with us.

Miss Bird would not have been in the room. She called it morbid, a sin against God and the truth. I suspect God cared less than Miss Bird who was mad for truth and disapproved of much in general.

I think Mother very brave to have acted out death with a husband at war and her own hold on life so slippy. She was never well but fragile, ill from the day I was born so you can imagine I felt responsible. Not that Mother ever mentioned it except from time to time.

Mostly she lay still and easy. It was all that could be expected. The odd trip to Chester, the shops, a little gardening, the occasional embroidering of place mats, such things were not beyond her. More might well have been fatal as she often pointed out. Miss Bird did what else was needed.

'Miss Bird', said Mother, 'is my public face.'

From time to time she'd talk with neighbours. They'd call round but not for long. Mother and the people of Cheamish were of different tribes. They didn't take comfortably to a woman who told them the wind carried diseases and Queen Victoria had worn tap shoes under her widow's weeds.

Miss Bird took callers into the back parlour and Mother kept to the front where the light lingered. It's here I see her when I look back and I look back often. On bright days she'd pull the green linen curtains and the room seemed to be lying at the bottom of the sea. Mermaids could have called on us.

Mother was by no means a stranger to the sea. Grandfather had been a sailor. He'd fished off the Cape of Good Hope and discovered an island off New Zealand so small it's not to be found on even the best of maps.

She kept his things about her. His was the fishing net draped over the piano, the figurines of serpents, Malay dancers and the genuine ottoman on which she lay. These were all I knew of him other than Mother's tales of pirates, kidnaps and black-skinned maidens on bone-white beaches. The rest of the furniture was bought new when Mother married Father but sometimes she'd forget. She'd point at the bureau saying it was from Holland when Hoole was nearer the mark.

By the sofa on a nest of tables (Parisian, Mother claimed) were her photographs. Grandfather was not amongst them but Father was, in uniform. Miss Bird was also there looking glum in a hat and gloves with me in tow. I was a lanky child with legs to the neck but Mother would call me a lump. She'd look at me and then her stomach and marvel how her tiny womb had brought forth a thing the weight and size of me.

There was but one photograph of herself. Looking lovely in a black moiré dress and turban she was reeling back in mock-horror from a spindly man in pants and a bolero. It was signed 'To Gretta from Presto, Con Amore XXX'.

'From my days on the stage.'

In Middlesbrough she had partnered Mr Nigel Costello, Daphne to his Victor, in *Love's Proud Boast*. When she'd sung 'To Thine Own Self Be True' drunken millworkers with no ear for music had stood up and sung along with her. A future of fame and brilliance had awaited her but she had given it all up for Presto.

'Presto, Presto, Con Amore Presto! A magician. A *conjurioso serioso*. No trickster. The best of his generation. We all said so. I caught his act one Sunday in Buxton, a charity do. He caught my eye as I sat in the box. He called me down to saw me in half.'

'And did he really saw you in half?'

'He sawed me quite in two. I felt a definite draught about my midriff but no pain. The audience were wild, savage in their applause and Presto whispered in my ear, 'Signorina, stay.'

'He spoke English, then?'

'Oh yes, he was Salford-born but his colouring was very Continental. I was his assistant for two years until he fell under a tram in Macclesfield. Sliced in two which is something like justice, but without him I was left bereft. Until your father found me.'

How Father found Mother I was never to know for certain. Father never said and Mother said too much and seldom the same thing twice. She told such stories. They grew up around her like leaves that decorated and disguised her.

One version had it that she returned to the stage in a non-singing *La Bohème*.

'It's cheaper without an orchestra. It took hardly an

6

hour to perform and, as we'd been double booked with some acrobats, we spun things out by having Mimi join a circus half-way through. No one cottoned on to how ludicrous it was for a woman with bad lungs to join up with a circus slap-bang in the middle of a big love affair. Folk said they'd not seen a Mimi die with such delicacy. One or two did suggest she might have been spared an early grave if she'd not done all that tumbling in Act Two.'

One of those moved by Mother's Mimi had been a young man one night in Parkgate. He'd stood up in the circle and cried out, 'Save her, someone save her!' That man had come again three nights running and then backstage to offer love, marriage and a villa in Cheamish.

'That man', said Mother, 'was your father.'

It didn't sound like him. It called for sudden passion and passion, sudden or slow, was not one of Father's strengths.

There were other stories. One was set in a TB ward, another in Oldham. One was set as far away as Venice but the details are lost to me now. I could see Mother in all of them but none seemed right for Father.

He was not a spontaneous individual. The fact he had met and married Mother was so beyond explaining no lie could account for it. A fact, sadly, is a fact. There's nothing to be done but hang your head and be accepting which is why I'm not fond of facts. Lies at least give you a chance for romance and a laugh.

The marriage must have been the one impetuous act of Father's life. He couldn't have given himself time to think. He never said if he regretted it but it's to be sure he did. Mother was no more suited to him than a compass is suited to make a perfect square.

He sold insurance because someone had to do it. This was his one joke but truth is he loved it. He was a grey man, proudly grey, thin as six o'clock, the dullest time of day, neither afternoon nor evening. His face in profile was almost vertical, forehead nose mouth chin and throat no more than a bump and a dip away from a straight line.

He was unbending. The world he saw was in black and white and what kind of world is that to look on?

I will try to be fair on Father as I will try to be fair to Miss Bird but this is an honest account. Time is no healer and my mind's not one for playing softening tricks. I speak as I find and I shall write in a like manner.

He did have nice hands. His fingernails were always clean.

An odd wife Mother made him, full and bright as a rhododendron blossom on the black branch of his arm. Miss Bird would have made the better wife but that would be suggesting incest. Miss Bird was Father's sister.

Bernadette Daley was her true name. It was me who christened her Miss Bird. My little girl's mouth wasn't able to say Bernadette without swallowing most of it. Mother made a grand laugh of it and the name stuck. The woman winced when she was called it but she never found jokes amusing. Wit in her book was plain malice polished up to sound clever. I daresay she had a point.

I never heard her laugh or speak overmuch in those early years. Later she loomed large but when I was small she was but a shadow in a long frock unnecessarily black. She'd churn out what few words she had for me through lips as thin and sharp as the blades of a bacon slicer.

There was some tragedy in her life, I see that now, some accident that kept her unwilling in Cheamish, some man maybe who'd left her there or who'd died on her, dead of pneumonia, no doubt caught in the cold clamp of her embrace.

I have some reason to feel for her. I have some reason to love her even but I don't. Call me hard-faced. I don't care. She had nice hands. I'll say that in her favour. She kept the nails clean and tidy. I think clean hands a virtue in people.

She hadn't always been in Cheamish. She'd been educated. She spoke Italian. She'd been to Constantinople. She came back when I was born and Mother had been bad with angina. She became the housekeeper though no one called her that to her face. She stayed in the back parlour or the kitchen where she'd arranged everything neatly and with an eye to order. Food was stored alphabetically and the pots and pans all had handles pointed to the east, to France and to the Front where Father was at war. On his return she grew more prominent in my life but still was distant. She'd emerge late evenings to spend time with him. They were very close. They'd discuss World Events in serious voices with the windows curtained and sealed while in another room Mother and I would play out some gaudy opera with the windows wide to a sky snowy with stars and rich with sea air.

Sea air was plentiful in Cheamish. We had lungful after lungful of it. What we didn't have was a sea. The sea had disappeared.

Once, and we are talking ages ago, there had been an abbey in Cheamish owned by a saint called Chad. It's said that this Saint Chad had knelt one day on Cheamish Hill and prayed so hard that the sea had come rushing over the land as if drawn like a twin soul to his tears. Saint Chad sadly drowned and was buried in Chester but the sea happily remained.

A saltwater estuary, Cheamish in its time entertained seals dolphins and once a whale. All this I was taught at school. For we're not talking small and narrow here. The distance between Cheamish and Scannell on the other side is half the distance between the Isle of Wight and France. If you wanted to go to Ireland in the nineteenth century – and a lot did, God knows why – you went via Cheamish. Handel did. He wrote bits of the *Messiah* while a storm delayed his boat. I think this explains why the work's so noisy. There's a Turner painting of Cheamish but there's a Turner painting of most places. Samuel Adams wrote his opera *Guy Fawkes*, very popular in 1890 but not much played these days. There was even a luxury hotel, walls the colour of ice-cream with a meringue-like roof. A tree grew in its lobby and birds sang in its leaves. Royalty almost stopped there. It was well on the way to being the haunt of the rich when the sea disappeared.

It didn't exactly vanish, just slowly and then less slowly withdrew. The tide went out and came back a little less each time. It silted up. Boats left from Liverpool and the White Hotel closed down. The tree that had famously grown in its lobby went wild and broke through the ceiling. Its branches scraped at the first-floor windows waving goodbye to the departing sea.

By the time I was born in 1909 high tide at Cheamish was a glassy zig-zag of a stream that had sneaked its way up from Hoylake. All along the promenade and out along the pier where the sea should have been was a carpet of mud and heather. Sunshine shivered in the puddles and the wind rummaging through the long grass gave it a look of waves but it wasn't enough. There was no longer any use for the prom, the pier, the quay, the ruined wedding cake of a hotel, the rotting breakwaters or the red benches lined up along the front like so many glossy-lipped mouths.

A sad loss the sea. I felt it deep. Even now I grow tender and lyrical at the thought, the way grief can make you do.

Our house or villa was on top of Cheamish Hill. From my window I could see how this marshland stretched for slow mile after slow mile to an horizon of silver smoke West Kirby and the promise of open sea.

I don't know how it worked for Saint Chad but it never worked for me. I willed that sea to come back. I willed it with all the force a young girl has and all the imagination my mother was bent on cultivating in me. I imagined it rushing liquidly powerfully foaming and blue, rushing back to Cheamish where it belonged.

It had left a hole in the very side of the town – and let me be fancy one moment longer – in all of us who looked out each day with a right to see water, wave upon wave of it, and saw instead only long grass heather mud and discontented seagulls.

I felt cheated but the sea ignored my calls. The sea cares for nothing and no one which is why I persist in so loving it and live now in full delicious sight of it.

One morning when I was eight Mother rushed into my room. Her hair was free about her face and her purple wraparound loose and fluttering with the speed of her. She was never a woman to rush for no purpose so I knew something momentous was up.

'Belle! Belle! Wake up, the sea's come back to Cheamish!'

I threw off the covers. I ran to the window to witness this miracle but there was no sea. I saw only the old familiar view of marsh and pink-frosted heather. Mother lay back on my bed and giggled at me softly. I felt disappointment settle in my stomach like a stone.

'It's not there,' I said peeved.

'Isn't it? It was there a minute ago. It must have come and gone. Serves you right for sleeping late.'

She rose from the bed and went to the mirror. She smoothed and tied her silk wraparound and folded the thick mass of her auburn hair into a swirl about her head.

'Sometimes I wonder if I've the face to go on,' she said quietly, more to the mirror than to me.

I hadn't a thought as to her meaning then. Now I read too much into her words and understand them less. I could say nothing in reply so watched her, entranced as always.

'By the way,' she said as she was leaving, 'your father's home from the war. For good, I think. He said something about it being over.'

*

They were in the kitchen not the dining room. Father was eating breakfast. Miss Bird was pouring him tea. Mother read a magazine.

'Kiss your father, Mabel,' she said as if she couldn't be bothered to do it herself.

Father kissed me back, his moustache drippy with egg. I wiped the grease from my cheek and he said how much I'd grown.

'And how are you getting on in school, Mabel?'

I said I was getting on fine. School didn't occupy me much.

He asked me to recite my times table. I think I heard Mother groan – or it might have been me. I did as he asked although I was well beyond multiplication at school and into fractions. I got to fifteen times fifteen and stumbled. I stumbled on purpose. I could think of better ways of celebrating a homecoming than standing minutes on end saying so-and-so times so-and-so is such-and-such, but Father couldn't. He found things like that entertaining.

'Said properly, the multiplication table is better than any poem. If you're ever locked in a room with nothing to do, it'll help while away many an hour.'

I said I'd bear that in mind.

'Wait until you start on logarithms, Mabel,' Miss Bird piped up. 'Now they really are interesting. 001. 002 . . .'

I said I couldn't wait. Mother said she preferred Tennyson. Sarcasm was lost on Father and Miss Bird.

Mother said she had a head. Her sofa was calling soothing words. Did anyone object to her going? I was given breakfast and forgotten. Father and Miss Bird lingered. They wittered on about war's aftermath and the role of insurance in a new time of peace.

'The Jews will do well, they always do,' said Father.

Miss Bird said she'd spent the past few months with her eye on China, always an unknown figure in any equation.

'A country not properly colonised will always cause problems.'

Father pushed back his plate and said he'd watch out for China but that it was good to be home. Cheamish was quite the best place to sit and study the world and its doings.

Miss Bird agreed.

It may well have been that evening I asked him if the sea would ever come back to Cheamish. A simple yes or no would have sufficed but instead I was told more than I ever wanted about the process of silting. In dry uninvolving language he proved what I'd not wanted proving. The sea would never come back to Cheamish.

'Never?'

'Never in a blue moon.'

'I saw a blue moon once,' said Mother. 'It was in Wigan,' 1904.'

Miss Bird decided to quote scripture, something she only ever did out of spite. She said in Revelation when we are promised a New Heaven and a New Earth we are also told there'll be no more sea. She said it with something like satisfaction.

'What'll happen to the fish?' Mother asked concerned.

'I don't think we'll have much need of fish on that great day. I think, Gretta, we'll be eating food a little bit more celestial.'

'I don't like the idea of that. Perhaps the fish'll grow legs and live on land. We could have one for a pet and take it for walks. Oh, Belle, draw us a fish with legs on and cheer me up.'

Why did Mother need cheering up the first evening her husband was home from the war? It's now in late old age I pick up on it. I thought only then how happy I was with Mother and me laughing at how fish would walk and whether they'd build nests in the trees with roofs on to stop the birds from eating them.

I've no memory of how Father and Miss Bird spent their time. With their eyes on China and the Jews I suspect.

I was my mother's child. I would have been even if my father hadn't spent four years away. Family loyalties just occur. They never seem like decisions but the way things are. I'd have sided with Mother for no other reason than her loveliness.

Loveliness was all about her, her face and figure, the soft swoop and cello of her voice. It was there too in the pleasure she took in life, especially its more morbid aspects. There was even in her darkest moments a sense of delight.

Father was a stranger to such pleasures. He never smiled and if Miss Bird ever did, her small pointed teeth made it look more like a bite.

They had few dealings with me. Miss Bird would plait my hair of a morning for Mother never rose before nine. Father would spend five minutes with me each evening. He'd ask what I'd done in school that day, but more to check up on my teachers than hear how I passed my time.

I'm over eighty now. I can see both my parents reflected in me – even a bit of Miss Bird sneaks in – but I lay claim to being my own woman and no more like them than a lily is like its roots. I have his face and skinny body with never the need for dieting. Life might have been kinder had I been given Mother's round good looks but as a girl the inside of my head was an exact copy. We had the same habit of mind and love of a good lie. I have it still but not as generously.

Her lies had verve and shape. They decorated the world whereas the truth as told by Father and Miss Bird flattened it. In their world thunder was caused by atmospheric pressure and not by angels moving their beds. Their heaven had no sea and hers had fish with legs.

No wonder I sided with Mother.

*

Not that Father's return was all gloom. Indeed there was a sense of awakening. Mother was roused from dreaming and I was wrapped up warm for day trips to Manchester, Liverpool, and, once, a weekend in the Lakes.

A car would be hired and off we'd go, Mother and me in the back. Father and Miss Bird would sit upfront, her huddled in the black wings of her shawl and him careful to go no more than twenty miles per hour which was slow even in those days.

Manchester was for theatre trips. They weren't successful and soon petered out. Mother was too critical. She'd insist we leave if she spotted an actress whose nails were dirty or if the smell of the audience proved distracting.

'Violet water,' Mother would shout over the noise of the engine as we made our way back through the dark, 'such a cheap fragrance, so common.'

Miss Bird would bridle but say nothing. She was a fan of violet water and soaked her hankies in it. Next day out of spite she'd smell so strong of it the air about her threatened to turn purple.

Such a lot of malice about. I was blind to most of it. I wish now I'd taken more notice. I'd have been better prepared for what was to happen.

Mother died.

She'd always threatened she would.

I was twelve.

It was in the midst of a conversation about lockjaw of the brain.

We were eating our meal of liver and onions so it must have been a Wednesday. Mother had eaten very little. She seldom ate much. She'd peck at her food and cut the vegetables into patterns. The end of any meal her plate was as full as it had been at the start but the food on it would have been more prettily arranged.

'Not eating, Gretta?' Miss Bird asked.

'No, I've an headache. Quite blinding. I think I'll go rest. Excuse me.'

She rose uneasily steadying herself by gripping the table as I imagine Grandfather had once steadied himself at the helm as his boat turned that nasty corner, the Cape of Good Hope.

The window was open. It was summer. The light was failing. A breeze with salt on its breath billowed the curtains. I was watching, alarmed, but my concern wasn't shared.

Father and Miss Bird ate on. They thought it was just Mother playing ill.

'What is it, Mother?' I asked. I wasn't supposed to speak at table. Father scowled.

'Nothing,' she said shaking her head slowly. I could see it was a lie. 'I dashed my head on a cupboard the other day. Do you remember?'

The wound was still visible, a red kiss on her forehead.

Miss Bird muttered yes she remembered and remembered too the fuss and the wailing Mother had made.

'I bled quite profusely and you all know I've not the blood to spare. I wonder now if I washed it properly. Tell me, Birdie, can you get lockjaw of the brain?'

Miss Bird didn't dignify the question with an answer. She sliced her runner beans with unnecessary viciousness.

Mother looked so woozy and still hadn't moved from the table. Her knuckles whitened as she gripped the tablecloth so tightly the pots and dishes began to shift and tremble.

Something terrible is about to happen I thought and then something terrible did.

Mother began to topple. Her eyes rolled back to the whites and then she coughed. She coughed once, twice, rather delicately, no more than a genteel clearing of the throat, and then she coughed again but this time it was thick and choking closer to a vomit than a cough. Out of it came a gobbet of blood the size of a small fist. It landed with a soft thwack on the tablecloth just missing the sprouts.

Father and Miss Bird looked up then but only to see Mother fall back in her chair quite dead.

It was a horrible sight. I can barely face remembering it. And in such detail too.

Mother, quite inert, was half carried half dragged up the stairs to her bed. The doctor took nearly an hour but I suppose it wasn't an emergency. He said it had been a brain haemorrhage and that they come with no warning.

Miss Bird said, 'Brain haemorrhage? And she always said she'd die of her heart.'

She said it smugly as if glad to have caught Mother out in one more lie.

Father said nothing. He may have grunted. He took the doctor downstairs. There were certificates to be written. Miss Bird followed thinking the doctor would like some tea.

No one gave a thought for my feelings. I was left alone with Mother.

They'd closed her eyes but not her mouth. I did her that decency and wiped it with my sleeve. I held her hand as it grew cold. I wasn't frightened. How could I be? Mother and I had been practising this moment for years.

Miss Bird returned, a black stick silhouetted against the landing light. She reached out and put her claw on my shoulder. I think it was meant as a tender gesture.

'Go to your room, Mabel. Let's be restrained in our grief. Death's a part of life and life is to be borne.'

Stiffly said, it was an attempt to console. She spoke what I have to call the truth. I went to my room.

I stood in the dark and looked out at the steely sliver of water that snaked its way through the marsh when the sea was at high tide. Mother had gone the way of the sea and I was more aware than ever of something missing and gone for good. The same salt breeze that had billowed the dining-room curtains now searched my face with ghostly hands. I shiver to remember it.

Downstairs the doctor had gone, milky drinks had been made and Father sent to his bed. I suspect death made Miss Bird restless. It didn't make her grieve. She's packed off the maid with instructions to rise early and sided the dishes herself. She'd pulled off the tablecloth and was holding it up to the light as I came in. She turned and showed it me.

'This blood's left a stain that won't come out without a fight. I suppose it's best burned.'

She was so abrupt and had not a thought for delicacy or me. My head filled with thunder at the cheek of her.

'No!' I shouted and stamped my feet.

I was twelve years old. Your anger at that age doesn't carry much authority.

Miss Bird just raised one eyebrow and lowered her voice. 'Don't "no" me, madam. If I say it'll be burned, burned is what it'll be.'

She crumpled the cloth into a bundle and threw it aside. All I could do was witness its sad fall. 'Mother,' I might have said, my voice no more than a squeak and Miss Bird so tall in front of me.

'The cloth's no loss. It was hardly the best linen. Other

18

things'll go too. Those ornaments and that dreadful fishing-net over the piano.'

'They're Grandfather's!'

'They're tat. All this room is, near enough. It's all tat and affectation. Your grandfather was never a sailor.'

'He sailed Cape Cod!'

'Salford Docks was as close as he came to the sea. He made boots for Timpson's in Bury. He had big ideas and he passed them on to her. It's all lies she's told you. I say this for your own good. She was full of lies.'

I must have been looking at the photograph of Mother and Presto. Miss Bird laughed. She opened her mouth and went 'Ha!' but there was no joy in it, hate more like.

'Presto was true enough.'

She admitted that with something like sentiment but she went on glassy-voiced and sharp.

'It was at a Christmas show at the White Hotel the year they closed it down. She went up on stage when he asked for a volunteer. She trampled two five-year-olds she was that eager. Anything to be the centre of attention. She held his hat while he pulled pigeons from it. He never sawed her in half. She was never his assistant. She hung about his rooms for a week to the shame of your father and the whole of Cheamish talking. She wouldn't leave him be until he posed for that photograph. She paid him to do it. And that message, "To Gretta from Presto", it's in her own hand. Have you never noticed?'

I shook my head to keep the words away. I was too young to hear this and too new to grieving to cope with how death shifts what's known and comfortable. I hated Miss Bird for being so callous but I knew what she said was true. Miss Bird always spoke true. She didn't have the heart for lying.

'What about *La Bohème* and *Love's Proud Boast* and Mr Nigel Costello and "To Thine Own Self Be True"?'

'What about them? What evidence is there? Where are the pictures? Where are the playbills and the newspaper cuttings? If it was true wouldn't she have them here all plastered over the walls? She was never on stage. She was a looker-on in a cotton mill. She met your father and tricked him into marriage with a phantom child. The oldest trick and just one more of her lies.'

She might well have stopped there. She might have held her peace and had her fill of truth-telling but the truth-tellers of this world, they have no taste nor pity. They think truth-telling's a kindness and they carry it to excess.

Or perhaps I provoked her. I stood fists clenched ready to defend Mother and defend myself for I knew, I knew what she was about to say.

'That was me! It wasn't phantom, it was me.'

I said it loud but without conviction. My voice failed and faltered the way it does when a lie dies in your throat.

Miss Bird sneered.

'You're adopted. There are papers at your father's office to prove it. You were abandoned and found on Cheamish Pier in a bag and a blanket like something thrown away. I know. I found you. It was me who fought to bring you here. What had she to do with it? I found you, she kept you. She stole you from me. I couldn't claim you, not being wed. Mother? I've as much right to be called such as she had. More. So come kiss me. Why not? All this I tell you for your own good. So come kiss me. Come kiss Miss Bird.'

She pulled me to her and I grabbed at her hair so tight I have the feel of it still in my hands, hot and dry. Her scream was a pleasure to me.

Truth. You can see why I've never been fond of it.

I made that up.

I lied.

Mother didn't die in the manner I've described. She passed on sudden after a long illness. Miss Bird nursed her coldly but efficiently. I didn't witness her end.

So why did I lie?

I lied for the sake of some pizzazz.

I lied because I could.

It's understandable. 'Mother died of a long illness.' Where's the drama in that? At least my version has some zip to it. Mother would have approved.

However, too much zip won't do. I had thought because this is my story I could do as I liked but that's not the way of it. I saw how in control I am. I can make and shape at will and have something like my revenge, but no. There's a certain power to be had in the telling of a story but certain responsibilities too.

Hence my immediate confession and apologies.

You'll hardly think me reliable if *twenty* pages in I'm already stumbling from the ways of truth.

From now on I'll just say what happened. I'll keep my sights on what's true.

What is true is I'm adopted. I was left behind in Cheamish by some day-tripper. It's not a thing to be said with pride but am I to blame for that?

None of this I knew until long after Mother was dead. I was told the week before I was wed. Miss Bird had run out of excuses for not coming up with my birth certificate and sat me down. With a nervous relish she told me of the sad circumstances in which I'd been found.

'It wasn't a brown paper bag like any other but one from Paul Henry Lee's in Liverpool. It's clear you came from a good home.'

I didn't believe her. There was a scene. Mother Dorothy my old headmistress was called in for support. She produced a newspaper clipping, yellow and creased, reporting a child left in Cheamish. It seemed the whole town knew but me.

My personal history was rewritten. This I had to accept

and much worse apologise to Miss Bird for calling her a lying cowbitch.

Not all the truth of my birth has been revealed to this day but as it's an event I don't remember I give it only the tiniest space in my mind. Mother was not my mother. This is a fact I don't let bother me. I keep her alive inside me. Her memory beats away like a second fainter heart. I look back on the past and I feel like spitting.

In the summer of 1925 I was fifteen. Father and Miss Bird went off to Italy. Mother had been dead three years. They must have felt it was safe to celebrate and Father thought he'd quite like to see the Pope.

They returned red-skinned and complaining of the heat but praiseful of Mussolini. Other couples would have come back with recipes or novelty goods, they came back with pamphlets in Italian Miss Bird would translate aloud to all who'd listen.

'Look, Mabel,' she said, shoving yet another photograph at me, 'it's of *Il Duce* in Rome. We were very lucky to get that one.'

I could see only a crowd of blobby faces with two pillars in the background.

'It's very blurred,' I said handing it back.

'Yes, well, he moved. He's a very active man.'

She wrapped the pictures in a silk scarf and put them away in a drawer.

In Florence where the drains had been bad but where there'd been some quite nice buildings not unlike the centre of Manchester but sunnier they had seen marches of highly disciplined troops and demonstrations of Italian might in air.

'It was most impressive. I can't imagine the young men of Cheamish lining up so straight.'

'And it's not a rich country,' said Father. 'Not yet.'

'It's not rich at all except in culture. They have a lot of that. Statues right there in the street for anyone to deface.' She added. 'They have beggars too with bowls no older than you, Mabel.'

She had a way of saying such things as if she were just cooing and passing the time but I knew them for the threats they were.

'You should be more interested in the world,' Father would tell me with a rasp to his voice. 'Develop your ideas and not laze about. Cultivate your feelings for your fellow man. Learn from your aunt and me.'

I said nothing. I governed my tongue. I'm not one even now for ideas and I've no more fellow feeling than could fill a sock. I think you best realise this and realise it soon.

I've had politics described to me but I understand it no better than a blind person understands a description of a rose. I had World Events and their consequences stuffed down my throat all my growing girlhood and I still can't stomach them. What was the world to me but something flat on a map with every country looking as if it had been badly cut out and shaded in difficult colours but some the same like pink of which there was way too much. I never saw the need to visit or think over-long about any of them. Never in my life would I drop a cup or come home early from work because Japan had invaded China. Miss Bird and Father did both the second they found out although they seemed to have talked of nothing else for years.

'I said to keep an eye on China, do you remember?'

'You did, Bernadette, you did. Well, the League is in ruins now and no mistake.'

I'd been told upward of umpteen times but I couldn't tell you what the League was or did. As for Japan it was a country where folk wore dressing gowns didn't use cutlery and built cemeteries for cats, and cats I've never liked.

*

23

I daresay I was a trial to them both but her especially. When I got sick and needed tending she thought I did it for spite. She treated me not with cruelty but spoonful on spoonful of castor oil, her cure-all. She made sure I wasn't in bed long. Once or twice in her presence and on a whim I'd stop breathing hoping she'd think me dead and be sorry. I wanted her attention I suppose but mostly I wanted to frighten her.

I was an odd child. I'd wake up some mornings and count to five to prove I'd not gone mad in the night.

She said it was to stop me moping that she instituted a regime but it was done to belittle me. I was allocated rooms to dust and vegetables to peel and prepare. Saturday meals were entirely my responsibility. From Mother's princess I became Miss Bird's skivvy.

The first time it happened quite rightly I protested. I said no way was I dipping my hands in a sink except to wash them and as for dust and vegetables hadn't we a girl paid to look after things like that?

She didn't argue. She had no need. She brought me before Father.

He sat straight-backed on the sofa in the parlour shorn now of all fripperies such as fishing-nets and figurines and cut flowers which had been declared morbid for who wants to see things dying in a vase?

'What your aunt says, you do,' was his grand final and only comment before flapping open his newspaper ironed smooth for him each day by Miss Bird and from now on me.

Far be it from me to sound like Jane Eyre but it's not a childhood I've a taste for reliving.

School was hardly a help. I wasn't the popular sort and when you're not the popular sort you can never put your finger on quite why. One girl said I gave the impression of being too good and believing no one else was quite good enough. About this I cannot say or argue. I just never had the knack of making a whole roomful of people love me. I was one who sat alone at a double desk.

It was a convent school and quite advanced academically. It had a physics lab and lockers for coats. Mother Dorothy made certain we were all for The Lord The Virgin and Benito Mussolini. We spent more time than was vital on Italian history and were often reminded of the sad fact that Jesus had been killed by Jews.

The nuns loved Father and Miss Bird. Mother they'd never liked. She'd seldom been to church and only turned up at fêtes to pass comment on the refreshments. Father was one of those parents who donated thirty guineas for a painting hung up in the hall of Mussolini crossing a field with the Pope and sowing the seeds of peace. Miss Bird lectured the Upper Sixth on Italy with slides.

'Thank you so much, Miss Daley, you've given us a portrait of the real Italy. Clap, girls, clap!'

The nuns paid mind only to those parents rich enough to contribute to their upkeep and the anti-Bolshevik fund. Father had money, not much but enough to make a rattle in a collection box, which is why words like 'sweet' and 'valiant' appeared on my reports for subjects like geography when all I could do was composition and housekeeping. When he stepped down from being a governor and Miss Bird took over I became ever more the object of the nuns' cold affection.

Poor girls were only noticed when someone died. There was a tradition in Cheamish of them marching in funerals, candles in hand. The nuns charged dearly for the privilege and only the rich could afford it. It wasn't an easy job. Cheamish had no sea but it had sea winds. Walking along the prom shielding a candle was skilled work but the girls would get tips from individual mourners. They'd spend it on sweets when soap would have been a better investment.

Being well off I never marched or mixed with the poor

girls. I'd watch them in class. I'd notice their grubby socks and black-rimmed nails. I'd watch the rich girls too, girls like me whose fathers had phones but who never rang me.

I watched but didn't belong. Between me and the world was like a pane of glass, and I was no more than an audience or better still a spy.

Some nights I'd go alone down to the prom. The sky would be lost behind clouds but now and then stars would flash through like sparks in the fog. There'd be moon enough to bleach the White Hotel the colour of clean bone and paint pearl the whole of Cheamish.

I'd crouch in the long grass and watch couples courting or the birds skip rise and dive in search of saltwater.

I'd feel so bitter and unwanted I'd ache with it. I'd fall to my knees and pray aloud my words rippling like silk on the cold air. I'd pray for the sea to come back to Cheamish and cover it all and everyone living there but for me. I'd watch them splash and drown flounder and call out to me but I would be an island complete in myself and wanting only the water lapping about me for company's sake.

It was a foolish prayer. It never came true. Why should it have done? The sea had no reason to care for me.

After so long playing Ugly Duckling to Mother's Dying Swan Miss Bird had preened her feathers to advantage.

Being a school governor added lustre to her crown at the Women's Institute. They'd come sit in our parlour eating cakes I'd made and clucking, 'Bernadette, what did we do before you came? You must take over the Bring and Buy.'

A Mrs Moss with a son at Oxford and a husband at the Bar was the real power. She didn't take well to Miss Bird's rise. Miss Bird herself found she was not content to remain one high-pitched voice among several. After years simmering in the kitchen she wanted no less than a leading part. She pronounced the WI essentially trivial.

At Father's insistence she started a select group that met alternate Wednesdays. They called themselves the Society of Concerned Britons presumably because Miss Bird couldn't spell Fascist.

Such evenings began with Miss Ellaby from next door banging out a hymn to Mussolini on the piano.

> *Duce, Duce*, when the time comes
> Who will know how to die for you.

They soon dropped that. Dying for the *Duce* was deemed too extreme an activity and although the tune was lovely the words didn't quite scan. Father suggested 'In an English Country Garden'.

It was not a very distinguished set. There was Father Miss Bird a few nuns and some people from the middle ranks of life who came for the company as much as the politics.

It was at heart a Mosley fan club. The man didn't just appeal to East End thugs but had a wide and genteel following on account of his good looks and dress sense. I thought he looked like Clark Gable gone wrong but Miss Bird was very keen on his black shirts. Smart but inexpensive she said they were well within the pocket of the unemployed and so poverty was no excuse for not following his teachings. The group almost succeeded in getting him to address a meeting until he discovered they numbered no more than twelve and decided not to waste his eloquence on so few.

'He's written us a lovely letter,' Miss Bird told them as if in consolation.

I was passing tea out at the time and made sure some splashed on it. As we had company Miss Bird could only trill that 'Really, it's quite all right.'

She later framed it, tea stains and all, and put it on the

nest of tables where the photograph of Mother and Presto had once stood.

As Miss Bird stretched her wings, more and more of the household responsibilities fell my way. I didn't complain. It was like my revenge. Done to demean me, it turned out otherwise. I had and have it still a talent for housewifery. These skills aren't instinctive in everyone but I have them in abundance. Miss Bird soon saw the usefulness of giving me a free hand.

Gone were the rhubarb pies with fillings the consistency of soup. My pies were firm, the pastry buttery almost baroque. One week Father insisted on my rabbit and Bovril stew three nights in a row. Admiring my cooking was his one way of showing affection but I'd long since hardened my heart to him. His compliments made no impression.

Miss Bird and I had swapped places. She had the parlour, me the kitchen. It suited us both. The kitchen rightly seen is a place of power and a better bolthole than school had ever been.

School I left without a certificate. Father begged me to stay on. Only common girls left early. Miss Bird came to my aid and made him see the sense of my leaving. My haddock mould bread sauce and boiled fruit pudding were produced as evidence. The nuns were upset to see me go but Miss Bird was determined to stay a governor and Father assured them he'd keep up his donations. They soon stopped mourning my absence.

I was given a girl to help me in the house. She'd been four years above me at school, one of the poor ones. She had a certificate but she took orders from me well enough. If she got lippy I'd give her a smack and remind her who decided the size of her wages. She was a sulky piece of work but I believe I had her respect.

I can't quite call to mind her name.

*

28

Miss Bird took to calling herself a *Femina Moderna*. Anything Italian was all the rage with her. Squawks of '*Azione! Azione!*' and lines like '*Credere Obbedire Combattere!*' brought back sad echoes of Mother's 'Presto', echoes that made the breath catch in my throat and must have made Father shudder.

At the school she started what she called a *Ballila*, a sort of Fascist Girl Guides. They didn't do much but march up and down holding flags. I daresay the poor girls found it useful practice for funerals but it didn't satisfy Miss Bird's ambitions.

She hit on the idea of going to work with Father. This was part of being a *Femina Moderna* but Father wasn't keen. She got herself a coat made to match his suit and a toque as black as his bowler. He said she could come if she restricted herself to filing cabinets. She went with him twice a week to Chester where they ruled side by side the wonderful world of insurance.

Never had I known such peace. Even those days she was in Cheamish she'd be elsewhere than the villa. There was her *Ballila* and school governors meetings. She gave talks to the WI on 'The Working Woman' and on 'The Housewife and the Free Market Economy' to the Society of Concerned Britons which was growing greatly. Members came from as far away as Kirby.

She was meeting the world while I was evermore withdrawing from it. The world had never held much interest for me and yet I was encouraged to have opinions on it.

'And how do you think this new man Hitler will act?' Father would ask smothering with salt a pork chop I'd slow-boiled the whole day.

'I don't know,' I'd answer. 'I've never seen any of his films.'

It wasn't the wittiest of replies but there's few things more pleasant than being wilfully ignorant.

I felt about Hitler as I felt about Mussolini, sick to the back teeth. Hitler I was fond of for a time but only while it suited my purposes. Mussolini I never liked until lately I learned what a liar he was. He'd say things like he had an army of five million when less than a million was nearer the mark. He picked the number out of the air and liked it so much he came to believe it. Now he seems an odd idol for Father and Miss Bird but he and Mother would have made a lovely couple. I like to think of him in Salo, a little bit of Italy Hitler let him keep. It was his tiny kingdom and even that he lost.

I feel for him there. I too had a kingdom and know what it is to lose it.

I kept house with an easy grace and as far from politics as possible. Some days there'd be when my only contact with the pair of them was when I spat on their spoons before laying the table. I was getting close to twenty-three with no hope of living better when Joey Bancroft came my way.

Joey wasn't a complete stranger. I'd known him a year or so before we spoke face to face and by ourselves. He was a wavery tenor in the Cheamish Chorale. I'd begun going there when I found they rehearsed the same nights the Society met in our parlour. Miss Bird had objected to my going but could see I needed an interest in life although she'd rather it had been Fascism than singing.

Joey was tall and so stood at the back. I've never been short and me and two other mezzos were put up there with him.

For months it was just looks and nothing said. I'd watch how his Adam's apple would tremble in the upper register which is strange for Adam's apples have never been my taste.

It's funny the things that draw you to a person. His gawkiness too caught my attention. He could never wear a shirt so it looked like his. His bony wrists were forever on show but long arms are a problem that can't be corrected and must be suffered. I overlooked them when possible.

No Adonis and nearer fifty than forty although age mattered less in those days he wasn't the man I'd made out for myself in my head yet still my heart tumbled when he took to passing the house in the hope of seeing me in the garden.

The washing I did that summer and the number of sheets I pegged on that line just so I could be where he could see me. My hands were red raw until I hit on the idea of Marjory – that was her name – doing most of the laundry and I just hung it out to dry.

'Hello,' he'd say shyly doffing his cap and moving on. He was ever a man of few words but I saw his eye linger over me longer than is normal.

His family came from Sandown but had long left it. He'd been bred in Basildon and had a business there until war came. He'd won a VC and lost an eardrum – popped it at Ypres but he never talked of it.

'Is that why your tenor's so wavery?' I asked.

'Eh?' he said.

After the war he needed the company of his fellow man and so joined the fire brigade. Happy times, he'd say and his eyes would mist. He'd left under a cloud but was foggy as to why. He said firemen weren't held at the very pinnacle of respect and the pay was a poor cop too. He turned to sail-making for the navy. This gave him a rolling gait and a liking for beards but it wasn't a skill you could use in civilian life. He was given a pension for his ear and ended up in Cheamish. He'd seen postcards of the place but they must have been old for they showed it in sea-filled days.

'Where is it?' he asked Mrs Spriggs his landlady the day he came.

She told him straight. 'It's gone.'

Disappointed but resigned – a catch-all description of my Joey – he decided to stay and wait until his aunty in

Sandown died. She had a hotel and had promised it him in a will.

These things I learned across the years but mostly on our walks on the prom.

'So some day you'll up and leave?' I asked.

'Some day.'

'And go to Sandown?'

'Sandown, yes.'

'Is there much in the way of a sea in Sandown?'

'Sandown? Lots of sea, girl, nothing but.'

'If you go,' I said, 'will you take me with you?'

I swear to God I muttered this but popped ear or not he turned to me and said, 'Who else would I take, you silly tart?'

From that day on it was clear to all that Joey and me were walking out.

There was nothing said against it at the villa.

Miss Bird was glad to see me partnered. She wished me well out loud. She kissed me and even wept to think how she was losing me. We both knew it was all for show. She said Joey's great age was probably a virtue.

Father was miffed to have a son-in-law his senior. Joey was one up on him in having a VC but they shook hands as if they were friends. Joey turned down an invite to join the Society. He said it clashed with choir.

I was very proud of his reply.

I thought it boded well.

It was not a big romance. Only film stars had them. Joey's ear didn't make amorous murmurs easy and I had only a theoretical knowledge of the intimacy areas.

Miss Bird took it upon herself to explain using diagrams

of rabbit interiors. The diagrams looked like the weather charts in the *Daily Express* and much of the labelling was lost on us both. After saying as far as she could what was what and where it slotted in she added that it was a very beautiful experience. This I decided to doubt for no other reason than the recommendation came from her.

'I'm so glad you've waited until your marriage bed to get rid of the precious jewel of your virginity. Some girls don't. They fall. The consequences haunt them all their days.'

That night I made Joey take me down the long grass like any other courting couple to get the business over. It wasn't like the diagram of rabbits. It was hairier for one thing, all lump gristle and dangle. The body was not one of God's priorities.

I'm not averse to passion. I've been in its grip from time to time. It's not unpleasant. That said, just give me someone who lets me be, not one who faffs me about with lovey-dovey words easy said and not to be believed. No, give me someone kind, who sleeps still and doesn't hog the blankets. Each night of my married life Joey and I would lie like figures on a tomb unless we couldn't help it.

More marriages should be like ours.

Despite the evening in the long grass I wore white with a good conscience. I remember throwing my bouquet and Marjory the maid grabbing at it – she always wanted something for nothing – but the wind picked it up and it landed in the path of a dog who carried it away like a bone.

That night we went to Manchester. We took in a show and had a room in the Mansfield Hotel. Father had given us money for a trip to Italy but we needed it for our business plans.

Joey's aunty had died a fortnight before and come spring we'd live in Sandown.

'Where is Sandown exactly?' I asked him for I'd been working up to the question not expecting her to die so soon.

Joey showed me on the map this island like a flake of land so small a wave could cover it.

'Oh,' I said, 'it is by the sea.'

'By the sea?' laughed Joey. 'It's in it!'

2

We travelled first class to Portsmouth, the tickets a gift from Miss Bird. She came to the station to wave us off in a hat with a black veil so folk would think she was hiding eyes red from weeping.

'I will miss you, dear,' she said honey-voiced and mock-sincere.

'I'm sure,' I said tapping my feet and eager to be off.

'I want you to know that should you ever need anything, help, money, anything at all, just write to me. I'll do all I can. I'll do it gladly. Cheamish will always be your home if things go wrong. You know that, don't you, Mabel?'

As the train drew away she reached up to squeeze my hand one last time. It was more than I could bear. I pulled my hand right back. She looked at me as if I'd slapped her in the face. She called out over the noise and the steam how she loved me, how she'd always loved me. She almost screamed it. The whole platform could hear. It was all for show. I shut the window and sat down.

'You should have been kinder,' Joey said. 'She thinks more than well of you for all you say against her.'

I hushed him with a look and settled back for the ride. I was leaving Cheamish and all such considerations well behind.

*

It was not the work of a moment to travel from Cheamish to the Isle of Wight. A long journey we had of it. Not till late morning next day did we cross over to Ryde in a ferry.

Now I know this crossing well. I've done it since one thousand times and more until old age grew me into a hoop and bad bones keep me where I am. But that first time is not one jot dimmed. The sea to me was like liquid glass. The sun spangled it. Green and living it was, wind ruffled and bubbling. It was true to every picture I'd ever seen of it and every picture I'd made of it in my head.

'Oh, Joey,' I said hugging his arm as we stood on deck the spray coming at us speckling our faces like tiny kisses, 'I'm that happy I'll burst!'

'Eh?' said Joey for I was standing the side of his gammy ear and he couldn't hear me for the slush of the waves. Not that he had much patience with fancy notions. The sea meant little to him. He may have made sails for the navy but he only liked water if it came out of a hose and was aimed at a fire. I enthused alone. I didn't mind.

'There you are, girl,' he said to me and pointed. 'Over there. That's Ryde.'

I could see nothing. The sun was up and the sea a glare. The island was no more than a dark scar against a blue and white sky. Then nearer to I saw it clear, a fall of green trees and red roofs stacked and sloping so close to the sea I feared they'd topple in.

'They call it the Island of the Blest,' Joey told me.

'We're going to be happy here. You'll see,' I said.

And happy I was that day and the next and the next after that. I was happy every day until war came on the island like a snake wriggling into paradise.

I thought war would change the place, change it for ever I mean. In prison I'd sit and worry over it. I'd think of that first crossing, of Ryde, of Sandown and Shanklin, of my lovely home, my view of the sea and my perfect, perfect life. I'd think how it would all vanish and become lost to me. Such things and worse happen in time of war.

I need not have feared.

When I returned from prison I found little altered. You see, this is the Island of the Blest. It's a fact I came to learn and learn too late. Nothing changes here other than the seasons and the traffic lights and then only very slowly.

It must be the sea that preserves us, all that salt.

We caught the steam train to Sandown but our new home was way above the town, high up along the chine. We put our bags in a taxi and gave the man a guinea to deliver them which was generous.

'We'll walk,' said Joey. 'It'll give us a better sense of occasion.'

For Joey this was something of a homecoming but I didn't know where I was heading. I saw this cliff path rise up high as heaven. Heights meant nothing to Joey. He'd spent half his life up a ladder. He said it was no climb at all but we had to stop several times to lean on the rail and catch our breath.

I'd have been right riled with him for making me tramp so far had the sight of the sea not calmed me. Mirror smooth it was and grey, the sun having gone and the day cooling. Cowslips and primroses covered the cliff face. I leaned over and picked some for flowers in a house give it soul as well as colour. My new home was much in my mind.

Half-way along Joey turned and said, 'Close your eyes.'

'Why?' I asked although I knew full well.

'Just close them, Mabel.'

I did as I was told and Joey led me on some yards further. I felt his hands on my shoulders and he turned me away from the sea.

'Now count to five and what'll you see?'

I didn't dare look.

I had truly been walking blind. I'd not seen so much as

a photograph and Joey's skills didn't run to description. He'd told me the house was sort of Chinese-ish. I'd imagined a place with walls yellow as cake batter, little slitty windows and a garden path like a pigtail.

I had trusted to fate which is seldom kind. I had trusted to Joey. I could have looked up and seen a midden but didn't. I saw instead the Villa Judapah.

A veranda ran round its pink walls and there was a pagoda roof of jade green, each corner topped off with a bobble of gold. Honeysuckle grew wild over the downstairs windows and the garden was luscious with bushes. Yes it was shabby and the garden out of hand but there was nothing a brush and a hoe couldn't remedy.

China had been its inspiration. Joey's aunt had married well and honeymooned in Peking but the husband had died young. He'd left her tidy but money has a way of losing value and she took to having boarders. The house became a hotel and she moved from Grand Lady to landlady. It wasn't a role she played with much conviction. She'd stopped having guests some five years before. She had arthritis. It wasn't an understood condition – or not one understood by her. She thought it infectious and hadn't wanted to pass it on to her guests. I think this shows she was kindly if stupid.

Joey and I toured the house. The kitchen was big enough to waltz in and the bedrooms had ceilings so high you felt like keeping your hat on. Each north window had a view of the sea and to the west was Culver Down, a soft lump of green cape and chalk-face.

Sandown and Shanklin were far below us. You could see them only if you walked to the end of the lawn out the gate and on to the chine. I thought that day looking down at the two piers, the prom and the tops of the shops houses and rival hotels, how easy it would be to drop bombs on them. The thought meant nothing to me then. It was an idle thing, the kind of idea that plays in your head whenever you look down from a great height.

That evening Joey and I sat in the kitchen. It was fully stocked – his aunt had thrown nothing away – but other folk's kettles leave a brassy tang in the mouth and by good fortune I'd brought one of my own. The electric was off but we set a fire in the range and Joey found a gas lamp in the garage. We sat in a halo of yellow light while outside the sky grew dark and far off boats called one to the other like sad cows in a field.

We planned our lives that night and decided the way things should be.

Getting the hotel on its feet was first priority. Up on the chine we couldn't bank on passing trade, not that there was much of it on the island anyway. It's not a place you just happen to pass by.

Joey was all for putting an ad in the *Daily Express*.

'Good idea, Joey, but wrong newspaper. We must think who we want as guests. Do we want folk with money or folk who drink their soup with a dessert spoon and blow their noses on the napkins? I'm entertaining none but the very genteel. I'm determined on that from the start. So we must think better than the *Daily Express*. We must think quality. We must think, Joey, of the *Daily Telegraph*.'

'Should we put "Under New Management"?' Joey asked,

I said no. 'Under New Management' sounded too much as if shady doings had once been the order of the day and had now been put an end to. I wanted no such stain on the Villa Judapah.

'What about its name, then?'

'What about it?'

'Well, it's a bit odd, i'n' it?'

'If it is, it's how I like it, odd and exotic.' I had an image of Mother flash in my head. 'The name remains.'

He didn't argue.

'As to the furniture, it's adequate. I'd like better. There's more chinoiserie than I think decent but we can chuck various vases and whatnots as we go along. In time we'll have money for more recent examples of interior design. The carpets will suffice but beds is a problem.'

'What's wrong with them?' said Joey who'd spent the early part of the evening jumping up and down on them and trying to entice me while I was busy checking the skirting boards for mice.

'They're double beds is what's wrong with them. They're clean enough once aired but I'm telling you now, Joey Bancroft, I'm intent on twin beds in every room.'

'Every room?'

'Every room. They're smarter and all the rage in films. Movie stars sleep in nothing else.'

'But the money, Mabel?'

'I'll wire Father and Miss Bird. That'll put her display of affection to the test.'

I had the money by the week's end. There was enough for four beds some navy sheets that don't show stains and some good crockery plain white with a gold rim, tasteful stuff. I meant to write back and say thanks but I didn't have the time.

I think in those days I was touched by God. All my decisions were the right ones. Joey came to accept this and learned to do my bidding. I was in my mid-twenties but all I did was done with the authority of one much older.

I had arrived, you see. At last I had some eminence. From being a lodger in this world I'd become a landlady. I felt it in me like a vocation.

I write 'landlady' now but then I thought I was a cut above. I called myself a hotelier. I thought myself that swanky. It was the newspapers reporting the trial called me a landlady. I bridled at the time. I bridled at most things then. Age has taught me humbleness.

Routine is essential. And organisation. I'd learned this in Cheamish. It's from Father and her I get this knack for efficiency but I like to see it more creatively as making out of mess and chaos a plain but pleasing shape.

Each morning I'd rise at five-thirty. The downstairs curtains would be drawn back but the blinds kept down in summer to save the furniture fading. Beds were aired and mattresses turned daily but those navy sheets could last near to a week before a guest complained. There were also chamberpots to consider and disinfect. I did these with eyes averted but you'd be surprised at what folk pass in the night. Ceilings and floors were swept weekly and Wednesdays a van came from Ryde for the laundry. I filled Joey's pockets with dusters so he'd know what to do if ever he was idle. I myself wiped each light bulb fortnightly. It's the little things folk notice.

We did have a girl from Ventnor. She mainly did heavy cleaning and vegetables but she was a dab hand at custards once I'd trained her. Her name was Dolly or Molly, I was never sure which. She had a cleft palate and I never had the time to sit and chat. I never let her wait at table. I kept her hidden from guests on account of her mouth. People don't pay to be met with a disability over dinner.

We turned a cloakroom off the hall into an office. Joey sat there when not busy elsewhere. Guests like to be halloed and farewelled even if only going down to the beach.

The kitchen was my domain. Don't think all I did was faff about with toast egg and bacon because if so you've never been on your knees at dawn raking out a range, blackleading bars and riddling clinkers. I don't think a day's properly begun if there's so much as a breadboard unscrubbed. Molly or Dolly would come to me with fingers near to bleeding but if a pan wasn't cleaned to standard I'd make her do it again. Today it's all press-a-button-stick-in-a-plug but let me tell you that in my day listeria was an unknown word and salmonella something fancy you did with fish.

I like to think it was my food established us. The ad in the *Daily Telegraph* made a point of it.

THE VILLA JUDAPAH
Clifftop Hotel with Panoramic Vista
OWN GROUNDS WITH TWIN BEDS
HOT & COLD EACH ROOM
French Cuisine
Shanklin 58

Your common man sees 'French Cuisine' and he thinks it means expensive. He doesn't come on holiday to spend money while your better sort think that's the whole point. I never had anyone lower than a postman at the VJ and he was responsible for all the mail in Glamorgan. He delivered none of it personally.

I cooked in plain English and only the labelling was fancy. I know no more French than I know Mongolian. The terms were sent by Miss Bird with hints as to pronunciation. Such lies are allowed in my line. I'd not get away with it now, not with supermarket shelves leaning more towards the Continent, but then folk liked only the idea of having *Bombe de Veau*. They were always relieved to be handed a plate of veal with an egg on top.

French food and an ad in the *Daily Telegraph* can only get you so far and that first year I admit we struggled. Joey had to work part-time as a fireman in Shanklin. He worked nights because I had less need of him then. He'd come in at breakfast with shadowed eyes and a stoop. Part of me wondered why I'd married a man so old and frail but good came out of bad as it often does. He phoned in the night to say the Raised Stag Hotel was on fire.

The Raised Stag was large and ritzy with a prominent site on the prom. It had a stag on the roof and was quite a landmark until that night when it burnt to the ground.

I pulled on my best cardie and rushed out along the chine and into the town. The sky was mad orange and black smoke. Already half the building and all the roof was lapped about with flames. A crowd had gathered about it. They included some who'd come by charabanc from Ryde just to see the fire. Planes were charging trippers three guineas for a thrilling view. Some folk are no better than ghouls. Only I paid mind to the poor guests in their pyjamas and bare feet.

I gathered fourteen of them and gave them two free nights at the VJ. Ten of them stayed on the whole week and four came back the next year. I had not a few others come on their recommendation.

This act of charity paid off but in the short run cost us dear. That winter Joey worked double shifts at the fire station and Father sent money instead of Christmas presents. I noticed it was Miss Bird who signed the cheque.

In summer we hired five bathing tents on the beach for the season at twelve and six each. We sewed a 'V' and a 'J' on them and rented them exclusively to guests at two guineas. The only time some of our guests strayed away from the VJ was to use them or play in the casino. The casino had a radio and a Johnny Walker scoreboard for the cricket but at the VJ we had most of the daily papers and a wireless in the lounge so they seldom needed to mingle with other holidaymakers. They sat under our trees as Joey served lemon barley in long glasses clunkfull of ice cubes it took three days to make. Evenings they could stroll to the Grand Pavilion to see anyone from Paul Robeson to

Twinkie but most preferred our lounge playing pinochle and listening to enlightened music on the wireless.

I drew my guests from the next to top drawer, that class of folk not rich but fussy about standards. If they like a place they come back year after year. Christmas they send you cards in the hope of special treatment next visit. Joey kept a list of their names and had a special hello for regulars but I'm not one for making distinctions.

I describe here my temporary guests. Any landlady of taste prefers temporary to permanent guests. A regular income is pleasant enough but a smile can only last so long. Even the best of us come to the end of our repertoire of meals and small talk. Your permanent guests soon exhaust both.

I was fortunate in having only the two permanent guests but then my two were Ayres and Gracie Ballantyne, a couple I could well have done without.

They came at the end of the season with nine suitcases an easel and a deck chair. I thought at first they were brother and sister and I'm still not convinced they weren't although I went through their things often in search of evidence.

Ayres Ballantyne had that heavy-lidded look no longer fashionable and a baby face that was ageing badly. The cares of the world might have wrinkled him more had he been bright enough to know what they were. I've little to say against him. He wasn't to live long and I think that colours my judgement but Gracie I never could stand. She had too many teeth and not all of them white. She walked about with her flat chest curved out as if breasting the tape in a hundred-yard dash. You longed to trip her up so you could have the pleasure of saying 'Aw, shame!'

Joey took to the pair of them more than I ever did. He was easy impressed by posh voices.

'This is absolutely quite heavenly,' Ayres said of the

view the evening they arrived. We were standing in the hall which has a view of the sea. 'It's simply the tops, don't you think so, Fishface.'

'Darling,' sighed Gracie, 'it's divine, essentially divine.'

I'm sorry but this is how they spoke. I think they got it from books and did it for effect.

Joey bowed and said 'sir' and 'madam' a lot which they seemed to like. I was just glad to fill a room.

That night there was only them so I served up hash and tinned pears. Buried Treasure was on the menu, a little thing I do with carrots and some prunes, but I couldn't be faffed to put on a show for them. They did dress for dinner, one of the rules of the VJ. She wore a *diamanté* cap that made her look much younger, around forty.

'I believe that this little place of yours will be a positive gold mine,' Ayres said. 'The Old Boot and I wish you and your young wife every success.'

'Thank you very much, sir,' said Joey.

I was also there laying out tables for next day's breakfasts. I sniffed loudly.

'It's so good to be away from smoky old London. At the moment it's simply *affreux* and the conversation too, too boring. *N'est-ce pas, vieille vache?*'

'*Absolument!*' Gracie cooed as if her life depended on it. 'The talk is all Hitler and, quite frankly, although I find the subject tremendously, even deeply fascinating, I've quite had my fill of him. This is delightful. What's it called?'

'Hash,' I muttered in the background.

Joey poured them more wine and out of politeness took an interest in what they were saying.

'Hitler? So what's the old bugger doing now?'

I have always told Joey never to use language at the table. Ayres blinked which was about as much as he ever did do in the way of physical activity while Gracie shrieked and giggled as if the word 'bugger' had been an ice cube dropped down her frock front.

Joey said he was sorry but she said it was quite all right.

One heard the word practically every day and she often quite liked to use it herself.

'So . . . so expressive,' she said.

I could have stabbed her with a fork.

'As to your question, Mr B.,' Ayres said, ' "the old bugger", as you call him, has formed an alliance with Benito Mussolini, the Italian chappie, bald head, looks as if he's been parboiled, invaded Abyssinia, you know, him. The newspapers are calling it an axis.'

'Because the world will turn on it, I suppose,' Gracie put in with a silvery bray. 'I say, stewed pears. Doesn't it remind one of school!'

It may be wondered why I present the Ballantynes so critically. I think their idea of dinner-table conversation suffices for an answer.

I thought I'd left such talk of World Events in Cheamish. I see now it'll always find you. Lock yourself in a room and hide there for ever. You'll hear it, history, the world, forcing open the window catches without so much as a beg your pardon.

I've never been fond of seagulls. Noisy things honking fit to bust outside your window the live-long day. If someone were to come to me tomorrow and say, 'I'm sorry but we've run out of seagulls,' I'd not weep.

Seagulls were not unlike the talk of war. Both disturbed my peace and there wasn't much I could do to muffle either of them.

I call these my Paradise Years but coming to recount them now I can't but make it seem like a news bulletin with World Event following World Event and me in the very thick of it despite my bestest efforts. I ignored it as much as I could. I was alone in so doing.

Some people they love a panic. They like to be miserable even more. There I'd stand with Joey behind me in the doorway of the VJ offering those who came a week in Eden. Leave your worries on the doorstep? Not a bit of it. They'd bring the world and its troubles along like they were just one more set of hand luggage. One woman brought four children with her which was trouble enough but first thing she says to me is 'Do you have a cellar?'

I said I thought the children would be all right in a bedroom if they behaved themselves.

'No no no!' she said stamping her feet in a right paddy, 'I'm worried about bombs. Don't you have any kind of shelter?'

'We've a shed in the garden,' I said, 'but the roof leaks.' She didn't stop long. Her husband was a dentist but you'd never have known.

I half hoped she was an isolated case.

I'd tell other guests what she'd said. I thought I'd been witty and I like to say amusing things. It makes me seem a character. Guests like that. It's good for business but no one would laugh about bombs. One or two got quite shirty.

'I'd rather see my children dead by my own hand', said one woman showing me the very hand she'd do it with, 'than see them bombed like they are in Barcelona.' She said she knew whereof she spoke. She had a sister in Cardiff which was not unlike Barcelona what with being built up and having docks.

She said this over dinner loud enough for all to hear. Her words fair upset me. When you're serving up *noisette d'agneau aux tomates* you don't want it met with talk of death.

*

This became the way of things. Conversation that could be so light and airy with comments on the weather sickness and cricket grew heavy with words like Czechoslovakia and Collective Security. Joey bought another wireless for the dining room. He said it was for the guests but his own interest was none too healthy. I'd tune it to light music when I could but Ayres and Gracie were forever leaning forward and twiddling it back to the news.

We did quite well out of the scare. We had not a few honeymooners. They seldom came down for breakfast but got charged for it anyway so they were good for business. If they did come down they had eyes and ears only for themselves. They'd not hear Ayres reading out the latest horror story from Madrid or wherever and they'd wave Gracie away when she turned up at their table with pictures of Hitler.

'Think of the poor Jews,' she said to one man who worked for British Petroleum. He'd told me when he came he was Methodist and not to give him butter. He could hardly be concerned about the Jews. I suspect Gracie of having been something of a Jew. She had lacquered black hair and a nose not quite straight which they say is a sign. She was none too fond of pork either.

I couldn't understand her concern or anyone else's. I thought this talk of war was the very thing to bring it on (and who's to say it didn't?). I tell you I was sick of it. When I heard Chamberlain whom I never liked – never trust a man with a moustache *and* white socks – say on the wireless how horrible it was to be digging trenches in public parks and handing out gas masks to kiddies because of some squabble in a foreign land I heard as well the definite thwack of a nail being hit bang on its head.

'Hear, bloody hear!' I said though I was spooning out creamed potatoes to a chiropodist and his wife at the time.

Ayres and Gracie tutted. They thought it quaint if Joey swore but not me. I couldn't have cared less. They'd not paid their bill for two months. I made a point of serving them last.

People may love misery but only in short bursts. They soon tire of it and we needs must smile. I was glad when talk turned from Czechoslovakia to Peace in Our Time. This is what I'd wanted all along and so to spite the doomy Ballantynes, cheer up Joey and partly to please myself I threw a party in the garden of the VJ on one of our few evenings of consistent weather.

Parties are not my line. There comes a point when you must leave go and your guests take over. I am one for keeping control. That night though I planned carefully and then stood back and let things be.

I'd laid out a buffet of tarted-up leftovers and had music on the wireless. It drifted over the garden like a slow breeze. My guests moved about in their best clothes as I'd insisted. Ladies in silver-splashed blues and pearl greys floated by on the arms of husbands neat in black suits and neckties. Oh, this is a dream, they said to me as they swirled past no more than shadows in the light of the lanterns hanging like gaudy fruit from violet ribbons I'd looped and threaded through the trees.

'Dance on,' I'd say. 'And eat up. It's all free and on the house.'

'And a beautiful house it is, Mrs B.'

That night my lovely VJ glowed splendid and proud and beyond this bubble I'd made of colour and fine music the sea hummed and the moon was a rose, white fullblown set loose in a navy sky.

'It's like a poem we're in,' I told Joey in a quiet corner and he snuggled close. He said I was the best wife an old man could want. He said he loved me though he didn't

51

always say so and that he was happy too. No more he promised would he talk of war and World Events. From now on it was just Joey and Mabel and the guests of the Villa Judapah.

The sad wetlands of Cheamish and the hard comforts of life with Father and Miss Bird were as if they'd never been, as if I'd never known them, gone from me and lost to me and good riddance is what I thought.

Then came a buzz like that of a bee but it grew too loud for a bee or any other living thing. It unfolded over our heads like a long roll of thunder until it became so loud I thought the very sky was cracking open. We all stood still and the lanterns trembled in the trees. Above us was nothing but noise. Then suddenly slipping through a hole in the clouds a plane came into view. It came spinning out of the dark and was followed by another and another.

There were four of them, four bomber planes heading for us with such a wind and a roar each one of us screamed and ran for shelter convinced that war was upon us. We scattered like petals in a draught and only Ayres and Gracie stayed where they were.

They waved at the planes like they were best friends long expected and late arriving.

'They're ours,' they called to us hiding in the bushes and covering ourselves in darkness. 'They're British. You can tell by the wings. Look.'

They all looked but me. My eyes were on the buffet overturned in the panic. A crystal brought with me from Cheamish lay broken in two, raspberry punch soaking the good linen tablecloth and turning the white bread sandwiches pink.

Next day I wrote to the Royal Air Force to complain about the noise and to compensate me for the crystal bowl. They didn't even reply. Organisations like that are indifferent to folk like me.

*

Summer ended and I was glad of the autumn rest. We'd done well but not well enough. Only one week in four had we had full rooms. Joey did weekends at the fire brigade and money came from Cheamish as a matter of course. They could spare it. Miss Bird also sent raffle tickets she was selling for Franco.

The Ballantynes lingered.

'It's so sweet here,' they said. They meant cheap. Joey had offered them half rates without my say-so.

I'd learned soon enough that with the Ballantynes it was a case of high tones and flat purses. Previous years they'd left to winter abroad but I suspect it was somewhere like Rhyl where it's cheap. They'd come back in the spring looking faded with Gracie's gowns having been invisibly mended so often the term had lost all meaning.

They had money but not enough. Gracie had a tiny income from an investment and Ayres had relatives who sent him a cheque now and then – probably paying him to stay away. I do hate those who sponge on others.

From what they paid me they could have found a nice bungalow. You can pick them up for near to nothing but the Ballantynes thought too well of themselves to live sensibly and within their means.

If I'd have liked them more I might have felt sorry for them. In summer they'd pass their days annoying guests with reminiscences of a glamorous past or painting awful dauby pictures I was expected to hang and other guests to buy.

Winter in Sandown was hard on them. They'd moon about the town but other than the library there's few places to sit inside on this island and not pay for the privilege. They'd get under my feet and I'd send them on errands to the shops. They were glad of something to do. When they came back I'd make a point of counting the change.

I made it clear they were there on sufferance. I banned all talk of politics but after breakfast I'd see them sneak down to the shed where they read the newspaper aloud.

Some mornings I'd come across Joey with them. I'd open the door and it was like an evening in Cheamish, all those Concerned Britons clucking over the world like it was an egg they were laying.

'Joey,' I'd say, 'come out of that shed and attend to matters more pressing. There's privet running amok and the drains need doing bad.'

I blame Ayres Ballantyne that Joey went into Ryde that Christmas Eve. I thought it was to buy me a present but he came back with nothing but the news he'd joined the ARP. They all said I should be proud to have an air-raid warden for a husband. Joey had expected me to be pleased. I thought where has he been? doesn't he ever listen to me talk?

We didn't speak until New Year. All Christmas week I'd go up early to bed in a sulk. Downstairs I'd hear the rivery murmur of political discussion. It was like I was still a girl and stuck in Cheamish and the years between had never happened.

I could have lay down and wept.

I probably did.

The summer of '39 was a difficult time. The weather never settled to a routine and neither did I. What's more, Molly or Dolly upped and left me. She said she was sick of my bossy ways and how I never gave her any consideration.

'Bossy ways?' I said understandably upset. 'If by that you mean my exacting standards, I'll not apologise for them. As for consideration, what consideration do you want? Love and cuddles?'

'A kindly human word now and then wouldn't hurt you. A "Hello, how are things at home?" every once in a while and not just "Clean them flues" and "Slice them carrots". I am a person!'

I begged to differ but was lost for words. Cleft palate or

not, the girl had a mouth on her and knew how to answer back. I blamed the talk of war which made folk nervous and upset the natural order. I told her she could leave at the end of the week.

'I'll leave right now, I will. There are jobs on the mainland. Southampton factories are crying out for girls like me and I am answering the call.'

'Well, they must be in a bad way if they're calling for the likes of you.'

She turned on the spot flounced out and left me with ten pounds of peas to shell.

I told Joey and he shelled the peas. He said it was a pity. She'd seemed a bright girl.

'Bright!' I said. 'She was as dim as midnight!' I reminded him when she'd soaked the aluminium pans in soda and turned the wooden handles manky yellow.

'Perhaps you're better off without her?'

'Perhaps I'm better off without the lot of you!'

I was mad that day. I was in a mood all summer and Joey was of no use. Every other weekend he was with the fire brigade on voluntary bomb alert. Wednesdays he was in a hut in Ryde prancing about with the ARP. He never attacked the garden with the same zeal and the time he spent with the Ballantynes made other better-paying guests jealous of his attention. I pointed out these shortcomings. I said the whole place was going to rack and ruin and I was being worn to a frazzle.

Joey said bomb alerts and the ARP were also things that mattered. The day would come when his country would need him.

I said I needed him more. Where did his loyalties lie?

September was hot.

'Hot weather means war,' Ayres said. 'Remember August '14. That was a scorcher, wasn't it, Tuna Features?'

'Do I remember August '14?' said Gracie. 'It was the month I met Sweetest Ayres. I was eighteen, everybody. It was too hot to live. Positively sultry. I was doused in talcum powder. When I danced I left white billowing clouds in my wake. It was too, too hilarious yet sad, so unutterably sad. I was young and pretty, my head was full of the most delicious fun. Two years later I was a nurse at the Front in France. All day and all night we'd hear the guns and cannons no more than a mile away. They'd bring in the casualties. They'd die. Some would die quite horribly. "One more good man gone," we'd say. We'd pull the sheet over their faces and refuse to think about them any further. There was never a time to weep although one wanted to so badly. "One more good man gone," we'd say and laugh, but laugh tenderly. So many good men gone. I think of them even now.'

Whenever Gracie grew wistful I'd half believe that once she'd been pretty although with her teeth so twisted and discoloured it was hard to credit.

DON'T LET HITLER SPOIL YOUR HOLIDAY was a headline in the *Daily Express* of that month. I almost cut it out and framed it. I'd have hung it over the Ballantynes' usual table. Many's the meal they ruined going over the news bulletins like vultures picking over bones.

'The world's really coming alive, Mrs B.,' said Gracie all sparkly in a scarf expensive enough to pawn and so pay the rent they owed me.

'Oh, gosh!' goes Ayres.

'What is it, sweetheart?'

'The gaffe is well and truly blown now. Listen everybody, today's headlines in *The Times*. "Full Cabinet Today".'

There was a general mutter of 'Oh dear!' I had my eye on a Mrs Kussi who was foreign. She had expensive hand luggage and could peel an apple with a knife and fork without once touching it with her fingers. She was of that exact class of guest I most wanted to encourage yet Ayres

Ballantyne's words had her dabbing her mouth with a napkin although she'd only that minute sat down.

' "Growing Tension", ' Ballantyne read on. He was tasting every word and loving it.

Mrs Kussi shifted in her chair. I looked at Joey sharp to tell Ballantyne to belt up but he was bent on listening too.

' "German Troops Massing".'

The murmurs grew. A solicitor and his daughter rose and left the room. I knew they were going off to pack. Any moment Mrs Kussi would follow taking her good luggage with her. I was near despair.

'And, I'm sorry, everybody, but this clinches it, this makes war definite now, "Nazi Pact with Russia". Germany and the Commies. Together they're deadly. Those of you with far to travel should go home immediately. When war is declared I'm sure you'll wish to be at home with your loved ones. It's going to be a bloody hard scrape.'

There was a silence broken only by Mrs Kussi's tears. She tried to get up but faltered and fell back in her chair.

'They will win,' she told the room. 'They will win. They will conquer all of you unless you fight. I am Czech-born. My family, I hear nothing from. I am so scared. What is to be done?'

I gave Ballantyne a look that would have stopped Germany and Russia in their tracks but it was too late. Mrs Kussi finally rose and wobbled tearfully out of the dining room to stuff her lovely clothes into her lovely luggage and never come near to the Villa Judapah again thinking of it only as a place where one heard bad news.

I could not watch and do nothing. I had lost Mrs Kussi and so I lost my temper. I had every right.

'Who are you to frighten folk and tell my guests to go home, Ayres Ballantyne? What if Germany and Russia are friends? We should all be friends and not wishing war on ourselves or ruining breakfasts some of us have been up since six cooking.'

I was blazing but eloquent. A round of applause was owing me but Gracie butted in before the guests could bring their hands together.

'But poor Poland? Adolf will walk right in there and take it, just as he did Austria, just as he did Prague. We can't allow that.'

'And why not? Who do you know in Poland? Why should you care? Why should anyone? Let them have Austria or wherever if they want it so badly. Poland's no loss to me. As long as I'm left alone, they can do what they like. I'd advise everybody to ignore Mr and Miss [I made a meal of that "Miss"] Ballantyne. Enjoy what remains of your stay on this island. I'll be serving lemon barley on the lawn come eleven.'

I had said my piece. I had said it well. I picked up some dirty dishes and glided towards the kitchen but Ayres Ballantyne was on his feet.

'Mrs B.,' he said. He had a voice that carried and an eye for audience. 'Dear, sweet Mrs B., you have such a blunt way of saying a thing, it leaves one quite breathless. It is in your nature to be so, and, ordinarily, we simply adore you for it. However, I don't think you mean what you've just said. How could you? I believe you say such things to console us, to soothe away our fears. Either that or you are deceiving yourself. Soon, very soon, next month, next week, perhaps even tomorrow, our skies will be filled with enemy planes. Bombs will be dropped intent on killing us all. They will spare no one, not man, nor woman, nor innocent child. This fear is not imaginary, but real. A well-rehearsed and executed bombing raid will reduce our cities to rubble. We are ill-prepared. We cannot ignore what is about to happen. We cannot wish it away. We cannot grow deaf to the cries of others, no matter that these cries be in a foreign tongue and hail from lands we have never trod. When we fight for a poor, benighted people against an evil so foul to say his name fills our mouths with pitch, we fight for ourselves. To concern ourselves with others is to be fully human, is to be British and to be proud.'

He sounded like Leslie Howard in the films. I never could stick Leslie Howard. He sat down to cheers from the others and I was humiliated in my own dining room. I was never to forgive Ayres Ballantyne for that.

Even Joey clapped.

Few guests remained by the end of the day. By the weekend we were empty. All reservations had been cancelled. Ayres and Gracie stayed on. They swanned about the place not even feeling vaguely guilty.

Saturday night the island was lit by lightning. Sunday found the four of us by the wireless waiting for war to be announced.

Joey and the Ballantynes let out a whoop of delight and then fell as silent as me. I just felt sick throughout my whole body, sad and proved wrong. I got up and went out into the garden. I thought a look at the sea would do me good.

It didn't. No sooner had I set foot on the lawn than sirens all over the island began to wail like neglected babies, long mithering howls. Out at sea the boats sounded their horns. Shocked birds rose up in clouds and added to the din.

Joey followed me out but not to see if I was all right. He'd heard the sirens and was looking to see if the Germans were coming. I told him he was looking the wrong way. I doubted they'd be coming via Portsmouth.

In the kitchen the taps were running and the floor was a watery mess. Disturbed by the sirens Ayres and Gracie were damping blankets in case it was a gas attack.

I was the only one who kept my head that day. I had the best attitude. I retired to a darkened room with a pot of tea and a plate of Barmouth biscuits.

*

The rest of the day passed in a doze. In the evening I scrambled an egg and went back to bed. My night was thick with sleep. I didn't dream. Joey kept to some other room. He woke me next morning with a telegram from Miss Bird.

FATHER SICK. SERIOUS. COME QUICKLY. PLEASE.
BERNADETTE DALEY

I imagined he was dying of disappointment, history not having gone the way he wanted. I wired back.

LOVE TO COME BUT SICK MYSELF. LOCKJAW OF THE BRAIN.
MABEL DALEY BANCROFT

I doubt they saw the joke.

I put down the receiver and stood awhile. Morning light always suits the Villa Judapah. It turns the hallway gold. I heard Joey's tread on the stairs. I looked up to see him in his fireman's uniform and two suitcases in each hand. He'd had them packed a fortnight since, hidden in the wardrobe, only I'd not noticed.

3

Joey wasn't alone. A lot of people left to take up war work or move to safer places inland. I should have gone too. It was just pig-headed of me to stay.

Miss Bird ignored my telegram and wrote begging me to come back to Cheamish. The Society of Concerned Britons was in disarray. Its aims had been misunderstood. There had been accusations and Father was ill with cancer. It must have been a fairly mild cancer as the hospital had sent him home, too busy preparing for war to deal with anything but emergencies. She said she was at her wits' end – not that she had far to go – and that Father asked for me often. She repeated again the things she'd said the day Joey and I had left Cheamish.

'Mistakes have been made,' she admitted, 'but now is a time for sticking close.'

I thought too right mistakes have been made, like preferring Mussolini to me. I was sticking close to no one but myself.

I burned the letter and heard no more from them. He died, I was told, in 1942. As for her, I couldn't be bothered to find out. Caring's not something you're born doing and I never had much practice at it. No doubt they both heard what was to become of me. No doubt I was discussed as they discussed other, more major World Events.

My business was finished. The island was closed to all but armed services and residents. I could give up all hope of guests until war was over.

I still had Ayres and Gracie but I no longer considered them as guests, more as parasites.

I'd have thought they'd have been on the first boat out, glad of the war but no, they lingered.

They wangled a form that made them residents and had some idea that house rules no longer applied. They brought their food from the dining room and ate uninvited in the kitchen with me. Ayres I didn't mind. He had manners and wiped his mouth between courses but there wasn't a meal you could give Gracie that wasn't sticking in bits to her teeth by the end of it.

Those first few weeks of war were thunder and slow rain but in dry spells Ayres and Gracie sat in the garden painting. They'd colour the sea dolly-peg blue and the sky would be a shade none too different. She took to adding grey clouds and calling her pictures 'The Coming Invasion' or 'The Threat from Above'.

'Well, Old Girl,' Ayres would say, 'this is all very cosy, but it's no way to spend a war.'

'Too true for words, Sweetest Ayres. When I think how we spent the last show! Such adventures we had. Did I ever tell you about them, Mrs B.?'

'Yes.'

'About my driving an ambulance?'

'Yes.'

'And how once we . . .'

'Yes.'

'Such stirring times. And now I'm beginning to feel they never really happened. Did they, Ayres? Did we really once track down a dangerous criminal – and get him! Is it true we rescued a girl and got hold of important secret papers?'

There were times when I thought Gracie could out-lie Mother.

'Now here I sit, a poor, tiresome, middle-aged woman!'

'I'd never have described you as middle-aged,' I said.

She turned and gave me a smile that was meant to dazzle but didn't on account of her yellow teeth. 'Why, Mrs. B., do you really think so? How kind!'

'No, I'd have said "elderly".'

'Oh, Mrs B., you're such a rough diamond! I wouldn't change you for the world. No! Really! Not for the world!'

The difference between Mother's lies and Gracie's was that Mother's had been convincing.

'But surely there's something we can do, Ayres? Something that's really *us*!'

'I've been thinking of Intelligence.'

'Have you, darling? How clever!'

'Well, I'm too old to deliver Jerry any physical blow but my mind is as sharp as ever it was. Sharper.'

'Mine too, Ayres Sweetest.'

'I could talk to Teddy Carter. He's always in the know.'

'Isn't he dead, darling?'

'Yes. Paddy Collier then? He was in the FO for a time. He'll help us out. He may have retired.'

'Oh no, he's younger than you are. Practically. Do talk to him Ayres, and mention me too!'

'Of course. Ayres and Gracie, always together. We're a team, aren't we, my Old Battle Horse?'

'Absolutely, and I for one don't want to sit out this war keeping a home fire burning and knitting bally Balaclavas!'

'You'd be wasted, positively wasted. They need women in Intelligence too.'

'In that case,' I said butting in, 'you can mention my name too.'

They laughed. I can't think why.

'Surely not, Mrs B.!'

'Why not? I'm younger than either of you and a bloody sight smarter.'

'But, Mrs B., that would just be too grotesque. You're one for the home fires, you're one for the Balaclavas. I'm sure you knit exquisitely.'

'I agree with Gracie, Mrs B. Intelligence just isn't your game.'

'Why ever not?'

'Because it's about maps and things, codes and documents and, um, things of that nature. I'm afraid it would be quite beyond you.'

'Yes, Mrs B., there's a great deal of reading and stuff of that sort.'

'So? I read. I read more than you. I've only ever seen you with a newspaper and then it's only the headlines. And it's six months since I lent Gracie that Edna Ferber. She's still not stumbled past page twenty.'

'But, my dear Mrs B., that is romantic fiction. There is no deciphering, no interpretation, no code to crack, no just getting at the very gist of it.'

'And, in the end,' said Gracie, 'there are only a very few jobs in Intelligence. I do hate to say this, and it's all very sad and deeply, deeply unfair, but, well, it's a matter of who you are and who you know. We know Paddy Collier. Do you?'

'No, but I know you.'

Even as I said it I realised this was no great achievement.

They disappeared overnight without paying their bill. I didn't mourn their passing. I was well rid and glad to be on my own. If war meant fighting alongside the likes of

Ayres and Gracie I wanted no part of it. King and country were welcome to them.

Poland fell soon after and some ships miles away in Scotland were bombed. Wherever they were Ayres and Gracie couldn't have been helping much.

The talk was all of imminent invasion but I paid it no mind. The island was put on alert but the only planes I saw were British. They buzzed about the sky day and night disturbing my peace.

Over on the mainland they had barrage balloons. Very pretty they looked in the sunset silver pink and blue. I wouldn't have minded one for the garden. A novelty like that can attract no end of guests.

Joey was in London. He'd come back for a visit if the mood took him or if I asked him. He didn't come often.

In November he had to come back to do my blackout. I couldn't be bothered to faff about with paint and brown paper and I'd been fined twice for showing too much light. If Joey hadn't come back to do it for me I'd have ended up in prison sooner than I did.

'Now they're up, they stay up. Don't you go messing with them. Do you hear?'

'Yes,' I said and that was as much as I did say. We had a very silent weekend.

He left in the night. I woke up to find on the pillow a bar of chocolate and a *Daily Express* Map of the War. I can't recall what I did with the chocolate but I put the map up in the hall. It had little stickers, flags of Britain and France and tiny swastikas. You were supposed to use them to plot the course of the war. I stuck them in any old how. They were forever dropping out.

The house grew large without him. It was nice to stretch out in bed but otherwise I could never get comfortable. I strongly suspect Joey was never happier.

He was on good money, three pounds a week two of which he sent me his own needs being small. He had a new set of mates and rushed around in a fire-engine feeling important. The engine was grey. They'd run out of other colour paint. He was leading a full life. I hated him for it. He slept with twelve men in a cellar the police had used for killing dogs.

December he brought a dog back with him.

'There was a pile of them lying in a heap. They were all dead but this one. His leg was twitching. I thought of you. He'll be company.'

I ignored both Joey and dog all Sunday. Monday morning I broke down.

'Don't leave me, Joey, don't leave me. Joey! Joey!'

I was most passionate but Joey was in uniform and eager to be off.

'I've been called to action, Mabel. It's no good. You must see that. I've got to go.'

I followed him out to the drive. He didn't even turn round. I was mad.

'Called to Action? You? You're an old man with a popped eardrum. Who are you to hear a call to action?'

He kept on walking, deaf to me.

Later he told me he'd not dared turn round to see tears in my eyes. I'd not the heart to say my eyes had been bone dry. I'd been too angry for tears and the dog was yapping in the kitchen.

The quarrel had upset him. He was a weepy thing with a bent walk and a whiff of corgi in his make-up. Truth was I rather liked him and I admit now to feeling lonely. Dogs love you without cause and without end. I called him Hitler. It was a name very much in the air.

*

You'd never have known it was war by the look of the shelves in the shops. That Christmas you could have what you liked in the way of vegetables but Joey was on full alert in London – so he said. I spent Christmas alone with the dog and in no mood for fancy cooking.

He'd sent me a letter now and then but he was never a hand with a pen. The price of stamps rose. I told him to write only when it was important – like if he was dead. I know it was cruel of me but I thought him too fond of the war. His efforts were all for it and not for me. I withdrew my love. It's a punishment that works well with dogs. Humans tend not to notice.

I came off worse. I couldn't write to him either. Still, it saved me a few trips into town. I'd not been fond of the new-style letter boxes. They'd been painted a gas-detecting paint, buttercup yellow and very ugly.

Mind you, Sandown was no picture. Sandbags muffled every shop. The library was lost behind them. They ran along the High Street like a second wall damp and rotting sprouting long stalks of yellow grass.

Nor could you walk along the seafront. The beach had been covered with great steely bushes of barbed wire that shifted in the wind and grew rusty from the waves. Any decent view of the sea was lost behind the mean grids of anti-boat scaffolding which turned our lovely strand into a prison corridor (and here I know whereof I speak). Also jutting out of the sands at regular intervals were rude threatening guns. It was well known to all that these guns held blank torpedoes and were only there for show. Barbed wire and lots of it was all that would have held the Germans back. They'd have invaded us easily with a good pair of secateurs.

In Shanklin the people who lived on the esplanade were turfed out of their homes so soldiers with bad teeth and worse manners could practise house-to-house fighting. Windows were broken doors smashed and good carpets trampled on with no thought that they'd once been people's homes. Breakwaters were used as firing ranges in full view of children and up on the chine and outside my house men ran back and forth swearing and carrying bayonets.

It was the British who invaded this island. The Germans would have been kinder.

Was I the only one to mind? Even the people turfed out of their homes seemed not to care. They said it was war and to be expected.

Sandown Bay was the best and only good landing place this side of the island, two thousand yards of uninterrupted beach. The distance is my own estimate but I daresay it's accurate. I measured it out with my feet on walks with the dog. I had to do something to pass the time. It proved handy knowledge.

The conversation was all war. This was another reason to avoid town. I for one don't warm to talk of lung gas blister gas and what-have-you gas while queuing up for bread.

People got such information from Lord Haw-Haw. They said it was chilling the things he knew. I preferred him to the newsreaders on the Home Service with their glum voices and oblong vowels but I soon gave up believing anything he said like how there were Fifth Columnists lying in wait all over Britain with electro-magnetic rays. Electro-magnetic rays! In this country? When you've only so much as to put a light on and you're feeding shillings into the meter every other second.

'Still, Mrs Bancroft,' said Alicia who did my hair fortnightly, 'you can't be too careful. The BBC said the Fifth Columnists are a very tangible threat. Or was it tangential? Whatever. It seems like they're everywhere but they look quite normal. You don't know who to trust. I mean, begging your pardon, you might be one.'

'Well, begging yours,' I said, 'you might be one an' all.'

'There you are! Who to trust? It's a muddle and no

mistake. Do you mind wooden rollers, Mrs Bancroft, we've no metal ones. It seems they need them to make battleships.'

I first heard of the Fifth Column in the butcher's. Mr Brewer could always be relied upon for a choice cut and I was a special favourite. I never asked for chops but *côtelettes*. He liked to have his meats translated but come the war foreign phrases were looked on with a cold eye. We weren't as close as formerly.

'There are five thousand of them,' he told me.

'Five thousand of who?'

'Spies. All round the country. Hitler planted them like cuckoos' eggs years ago. He's been planning it some time. These spies are getting paid upward of thirty pound a month.'

'Thirty pounds a month? That's more than our Joey earns in a year with the AFS. He's fighting on the wrong side. Do they take ladies? I might sign up.'

I said it for a joke. I think it helps to laugh with trade. He smiled at the time but later even this casual remark was to be used against me.

As was an event a few weeks later.

Two enemy planes flew down Sandown High Street. The place was in a mad panic with people running for cover behind the sandbags. I stood where I was and looked up. I even did a Gracie Ballantyne and waved. I thought I was being brave until Arthur Forman the greengrocer ran out and tackled me to the ground. His head was covered with the bowl he used for weighing potatoes. He called me a silly cow and asked me if I wanted to be killed.

I never shopped with him again and that wave, my one

bit of war-time pluck, was later to be described as signalling to the enemy.

German planes flew over regularly. They kept their bombs for the mainland (apart from Ventnor which had a radar station so bombs were to be expected). British planes would catch them on the way back and there'd be quite a few dogfights which I thought unnecessary, the damage already having been done.

Once or twice the planes dropped not bombs but leaflets. They came direct from Hitler and weren't at all ranting. I liked his getting in touch with ordinary people like me but I saw some rip these messages up without even looking at them. I call that having a closed mind.

A few careless words aside (such as telling the butcher I thought German sausage second to none) I kept to myself and governed my tongue.

It wasn't easy.

Out walking the dog one day a woman in a fussy jacket came over and said, 'Wear this.'

She gave me this red headband.

'Why?' I asked not unreasonably.

'We are enacting an air raid,' she said. Her voice had a proper bark to it. 'The whole of Sandown has been obliterated and you have been shot in the head. You're still living, but only just. Lie down and a St John Ambulance worker will attend to you presently.'

I wasn't lying down on the pavement for anybody and I told her so.

'You must! Be thankful I gave you a headband. Head-wounds are a priority. You could have had an armband or an ankle-strap. Limbs are a very low concern. Now lie down!'

She marched off and I sort of crouched for a bit. There were a few others down the street with bits of ribbon round them, standing still and looking foolish. I waited five minutes and saw no sign of assistance so I tied my head-band to a railing and left a note under a pebble: Have bled to death and gone home.

We stand alone, said Winston Churchill. I thought, Alone! he doesn't know the meaning of the word. He didn't have a business going to pot or a husband running free in a fire-engine.

France had fallen. There was a great to-do in the shops which was where I got my information. I no longer had newspapers delivered. For me they'd only ever been things left over from the day before I used to light the fire.

'It's hotting up,' said Brewer as he made up my meat ration. 'I can give you two chops. Pork.'

'Two chops to last the week! I do have a dog.'

I knew for a fact he had a drawerful of tripe out the back. Offal was now a luxury – such is war – and only allowed to the privileged of which I wasn't one, not since I'd begun expressing comments contrary to the National Spirit and arguing with soldiers over the placing of barbed wire. (There's no truth in the rumour I'd set the dog on them.)

I looked at the chops pale and limp on the scale.

'They never weigh enough.'

'I'm afraid they do,' he said offended. He stepped back with his hands up. The scales shifted but not enough to make a fuss so I clucked my disgust instead.

'There is a war on, you know,' he said needlessly.

'I had noticed.'

'You're lucky to get meat at all with the Germans poised

for attack. They're sitting not miles away on the other side of the Channel, sitting in their tanks ready to cross.'

I quite liked the thought of all those tanks crossing the water paddling along like turtles holding their snouts up in the air. I may have smiled. I might even have laughed.

'Anyway,' I said, 'why should you care if they do invade us? They're a meat-loving nation. You should do well out of them.'

I think what I said was sensible but war makes folk shy of common sense. They come at truth in a sidelong manner if they come at it at all. Those of us who say things straight, we never prosper.

For a time things fell off. There were still planes overhead but nothing like as many. War stopped feeling real and then Dunkirk happened.

I'd never call it our finest hour. Our Boys being dragged from France in paddle boats and pleasure cruisers? I'd call that embarrassing.

The island's ferry, the *Gracie Fields*, was used. It sank. The fuss in the shops next day you'd think the singer herself had met a watery end — not that she had a voice that pleased me. I prefer Dame Eva Turner, lovely breath control. She could swallow a whole orange.

The army used Dunkirk as an excuse to put up more barbed wire. I was more than a little put out.

You know how sea-haunted an individual I am. Walking by the sea was my one reliable pleasure. A good trudge by the sea with the wind wrapping itself about me was like having my too hot heart cupped by cooling hands. How was I to calm myself when my favourite coves had been turned into fierce gardens of metal thorns? I took to walking with secateurs in my pocket.

Open fields and the long green velvet slope of Culver Down had been similarly vandalised. How could I let the dog loose on land where the army had planted burnt-out cars kitchen ranges bedsteads and iron hoops the size of a small boy? It was done to stop enemy planes coming down but I doubt if the Germans could have done more damage to the landscape.

Such junk fair broke my heart but it was too heavy for me to shift. I tried more than once but there was always some soldier about with nothing better to do than tell me to move on.

'What's your name?'

'Mabel Daley Bancroft,' I'd tell them with pride. 'I live at the Villa Judapah up there. I hope the bloody Germans do come. They're a very clean race. I can't see them dumping rubbish in a natural beauty spot.'

'Mabel Bancroft? I've been told about you. You've already been reported twice for doing this. You do this again and you'll get fined. You might even get arrested for interfering with MOD property.'

I'd trained the dog to growl at uniforms. He was small but convincing. Soldiers usually let me off with a caution.

'Go home, you daft bint, and stop twatting about.'

Back at the VJ time moved like a foxtrot slow slow quick quick slow. There were empty days. I'd sit down late morning and then look up. The light would have failed and evening come.

I thought of Mother often. Happy thoughts. I find the dead good company once thinking about them stops hurting. I'd wake up at night with her name on my lips, my mouth shaped to call out to her. Only the dog ever heard. He'd come up from the kitchen. I'd hear him pad through the house then feel his breath on my hand.

I didn't mope. I'm not one for misery and have no talent for it. Dark nights of the soul are no hobby of mine although like most I've known some glum afternoons. Planes woke me more than dreams. They disturbed the dog. He'd whine at them like the wind at the door.

Having a dog called Hitler arguing with soldiers and not shedding a tear for the *Gracie Fields* I was very much out of step in war-time Britain.

I was made to feel it.

Alicia still did my hair but skimped on perming solution. Brewer's meat grew tough and skinny and we'd hardly cross two words over the counter. I made do with mince and made it last. Marvellous how mince strings out.

I was meant to care but didn't.

I still don't.

There are things I regret like never learning to knit not having a proper mother or close female friend but I don't regret not caring.

I was what is called now a dissident. It was the nation wanted war, not me. It was up to it to change.

In the meantime I was going against the grain but why else does the grain exist if not to go against?

Joey came back late September. There'd been an air raid the whole night. I'd not slept and was in a mood. Calm and rested the visit might have passed by better but he'd brought Gracie Ballantyne back with him. The sight of her did nothing for my temper.

They looked tired and dirty. Her face was greasy black as a darkie's but her lipstick was red and freshly applied before entering the house. (In such ways I admit she showed she was a lady.) Joey looked worse in his shirt-sleeves. Gracie wore his jacket over a white blouse splashed pink. The pink I learned was blood soaked in and dried.

'Well, Joey,' I said in greeting, 'it's nice to see you here and bringing guests. We need them badly but why bring her? She hasn't paid her bill from last time.'

I said it lightly but my true feelings have a way of sharpening my words.

'Ayres Ballantyne is dead,' said Joey bluntly. 'I'll tell you what happened later. Take Gracie upstairs, run her a bath, make her a bed, get her some clean clothes. Her suitcase is outside. She's done-in, poor girl. It's all right, Gracie love, you're home now. Mabel'll look after you.'

I said nothing. I was too curious to argue and so I did as I was bidden. I took her upstairs. I put her in one of the smaller single rooms seeing as how she'd not paid last time. She seemed not to notice much. She muttered a few thank-yous and took a great deal of time. She stumbled about the place bent-backed and stiff-kneed like a dining-room chair on the move. She looked for once the old woman she was. I ran her a bath – three inches – and left her to it.

Joey was in the kitchen his head in his hand the dog licking his muddy boots and him not caring.

I stood awhile not speaking only looking thinking this is my Joey why aren't I glad to see him back? You live alone for a time and the inside of your head is like a two-acre field. You gallop about it unhindered. Now it felt the size of a backyard and Joey was trespassing.

'I see you're on first name terms with Her Ladyship. Very cosy.'

'Make us some tea.'

'Tea's rationed,' I said. 'You have some now and there'll be none for you later.'

'Just make it, Mabel!'

I wasn't disposed to him ordering me about but once more I governed my tongue. I made him the tea. He didn't drink it. He just brought it to his lips once or twice. I watched it grow stone cold and pitied the waste.

'I've been seeing a bit of them in London,' he said finally. 'They had lodgings in Chelsea, not very nice ones.

I've fought a few fires up there lately. That's how we met up. We'd go out for a drink and a meal at this place in Soho they knew. We had some laughs. They were doing LDV work.'

'I thought they were going to be in Intelligence?'

'No. He was too long in the tooth. They wouldn't even consider her. Still, they done sterling work with the LDV. Everyone says. It's been bad, Mabel, really bad . . . so bad.'

My Joey cried that morning. He said it had been building up inside him for weeks. I'd never seen a man cry not even in films. It's not an easy sight. A tearful man doesn't take to being consoled. You sit watching him, wondering what to do with your hands, hating him for being so soft and making you feel so useless. I gave him a hankie. The dog gave him a paw.

'Ayres Ballantyne died two nights since. I've not slept for four. At night the bombers keep you busy and you spend all day clearing up. Oh, Mabel, you've no idea what it's been like.'

'We've not been exempt from bombs here, you know. Several have fallen on Ventnor.'

Some mornings I'd wake up to see smoke dragging the island like a veil. The smoke had a smell of wet matches to it and clung to the washing.

Joey waved my words away. London he said was worse. I said it wasn't a competition and what else did he expect? It was the capital.

'Bombs, they come down with this scream. It's like they're ripping the air and your ears go numb with the noise. You say several have fallen on Ventnor. Imagine hundreds. Imagine hundreds a night. Windows bursting and the street trembling like you're standing on jelly. The smoke climbs high as heaven and the dust comes at you, it covers you all over like a second skin. Like the devil it is, climbing in your mouth, up your nose so you can't think, your insides foggy with it. I was working alongside this chap one night and he was hit in the eye by some shrapnel. A few more inches and it could have been me! I watched it go in. I saw it all so slow and dream-like, a little spike of metal hitting his eye like a stone being flung into soft mud. Blood sprayed out. It hung before me like a cloud before it fell on my face. It was so warm, it was like bathwater.'

He lifted his hand to his face and mimicked the spray covering his face. His nails were rimmed thick with dirt.

'When did you last wash them hands?' I asked him but he didn't answer.

'So warm,' he said again.

Why was he telling me this? As if such a detail was of earthly use or interest to me. I wanted to know how Ballantyne had died.

'We were by the river in Chelsea. A kiddies' hospital was on fire and a row of houses in the next street, all empty, thank God. Bombs were falling stick on stick. It was so hot I know how a log feels when it's thrown on the fire. I saw Gracie and she was dragging some man twice her size on to the embankment. He'd passed out with the heat.'

He stopped his snuffling to chuckle at the memory of dear old Gracie Ballantyne. I clucked and told him to get on with it.

'I went over to help and see how she was. Away from the fire you grow cold. You're soaked through with water, see. Fifty yards from the blaze and you could be in Alaska. Then Georgy comes along. Georgy Aveline. He knew Ayres at school. He's a bank manager with a wife in Surrey but he sleeps in a bunk above me and shares my sugar.'

'That must be jolly,' I said. 'So what did this Georgy Aveline want?'

'He didn't want anything, poor Georgy. He tugged at my sleeve and said, "Over here. Ayres Ballantyne is dead." Round the corner a building had fallen, the whole front of it, like a slice of bread. Ayres'd got caught in the debris.

He was quite dead. Gracie heard us talking. She followed us. His face, there was nothing left of it. It was like old fruit, bruised and pulpy.'

'How did you know it was him if he had no face?'

'You just know a thing like that, Mabel, you just know it! She didn't cry. She just sat down and cradled him in her arms. It was lovely, really lovely. We left them for a moment out of respect and to find a stretcher. We saw him carried away and went back to the fire.'

'Gracie too?'

'Gracie too.'

'She went back to the fire with her husband fresh dead?'

'We tried to make her do otherwise but she said there was work to be done. Ayres would've understood, she said, Ayres would've cheered. He would have done, you know. It's the spirit of the times. It's how we all are in the Blitz. You should have seen her, Mabel. I was proud to know her. Valiant is what she was, valiant.'

Valiant? I saw red. Here was Joey going on like radio newsreel about plucky Britain under fire and singing hymns to Our Lady Gracie of the Blitz! I thought him morbid with his tales of spraying eyes and her I thought hard-faced, leaving a dead husband to fight fires in other folk's houses. A pig in a sty would have more sense of what's proper!

And was I meant to be sad over the death of Ayres Ballantyne? A man who'd done a moonlight flit, left me his debts and now was dead with no way of repaying them? A man who had humiliated me in my own dining room? Try as I might I could find no tears for him. Not that I tried hard. Not that I tried at all. If I was to weep I'd weep for myself. Joey had forgotten me. Where was his praise for me in all this, abandoned as I had been?

'So what are you doing here? I'm surprised you could drag yourself away.'

'We caught the midday train and stopped outside Southampton for the night. I had to take her somewhere.

Those lodgings were filthy and she'd have been alone. She's done-in, poor woman. She needs rest.'

'So you brought her here?'

'Where else was there? Ayres'll be here in a day or two.'

'Ayres?'

'His body. It needs burying. I thought you could handle that. He was C of E.'

'He could have been Buddhist for all I care. So I've to arrange his funeral? Where will you be meantime?'

'I'll try to come down for it. I'm going back.'

'I see. When?'

'There's a boat leaves Cowes at six and a train at seven. I have to go back, girl. I shouldn't really be here. I'm needed.'

'You're needed here! I need you!'

'What help do you need? You haven't seen what I've seen. You don't understand what this war is.'

'Don't I? I'll show you. Come here.'

I got hold of his hand dirty though it was and took him out to the garden, the dog flapping about our feet.

'Look,' I said and pointed.

I pointed at the hedge of barbed wire that ran along the garden fence and then at the decaying obstacle course of bedsteads and old cars that littered Culver Down. I pointed toward the golf course where in August a plane had crash-landed and left a scorch mark so large it looked as if God himself had been smoothing out the green folds and hills and then left His iron standing too long. I told him of the soldiers who ran past night and day with bayonets and the ones who'd taken up residence in the next field with an anti-aircraft gun. I told him how they were forever watching me and leaving their cigarette stubs in our privet. I told him of the dogfights out at sea and then pointed to our beloved VJ with its black windows and empty rooms. I showed him our ruined kingdom, our spoiled paradise. His tired face softened and I thought he'd understood at last.

'I'm doing my best with the garden but it lacks your touch. This hot weather brings out the slugs and you can't get the pellets no more. They say vinegar works but slugs lap it up and salt's too scarce to use.'

I was gabbling, I know it. I wanted my words to be as silk cool and flowing to wrap him round and bind him to me but he just said, 'Mabel, the Germans, they— '

'Bugger them, Joey. What are they, after all, but human like the rest of us? What if they did come? What of it? We'd be all right. We'd be fine. Why worry? People'd still need a place to go on holiday. There'll always be folk with money enough to spend on a room with fresh sheets and a view of the sea.'

'But Hitler's worse than that.'

'Oh, Joey, listen!'

'No. Hitler's like . . . I don't know. Hitler's . . . Hitler's going to come and he'll . . . Hitler's going to come and— '

'Don't, Joey. Don't keep saying that name.'

'Hitler? Why not?'

'The dog thinks you're calling him.'

Joey looked at me as I hope never to be looked at again. His face was old and distant. It was as if he was no longer inside it but had upped and gone ten miles away unable to bear what his eyes were seeing. Is that a way for a husband to look at his wife?

'You've called that dog Hitler?'

'Yes. What's wrong with that? I'll call it what I like. There's no law against it or none I mind breaking.'

Joey wasn't used to arguing with me. He'd not the vocabulary. He humphed and said God forgive him I made him sick and he went back to the house.

I watched him go. He looked so stooped. His little legs shuffled along as he hurried away from me. My old fondness for him came back. He was too old to be fighting fire or me. He was my husband and I loved him but then he poked his head out of the kitchen window and called out to me.

'I had to walk away. I couldn't find words fit to describe you but now I can.'

'Oh yes?' I called back. 'What words are these, pray tell? And where did you find them? On the kitchen table? Or did you rush upstairs to Lady Muck in her bath? Or in her bed? Is that the game you've been playing?'

I wasn't making sense. I said what I feared not what I thought was true.

'Don't you say such things about her. That woman is the salt of the earth and worth ten of you.'

'It's nice to hear you defend *her* yet you stick your head out the window to yell words against me. Well, what are these words you've found?'

'I've forgotten them now!'

'Forgot? You're wet, you are. You're wet and you're weedy and you're no use. You never have been. You're old flesh, Joey Bancroft. Go back to London, go on. I hope a bloody bomb drops on you. Then I'll have a word that describes me perfectly, I'll be Joey Bancroft's widow!'

Joey said nothing. He just closed the window very slowly. I stayed in the garden fuming. I'd have stayed there until he'd gone but the dog was upset with all the rowing. He was barking fit to bust and one of the soldiers in the next field was leaning back on the grass and laughing.

I went back in.

Joey was upstairs. I could hear water gurgling in the pipes. I banged about the kitchen trying to calm down but it was no good. In the end I grabbed my coat and handbag from the hall, picked up the lead and took the dog out for a walk.

Little did I think it was my destiny I was setting out to meet.

*

I've not a mystical nature. I'm on friendly terms with God – we chat now and then – but He doesn't soothe my soul the way a long walk in sight of the sea never fails to do. How can you not be moved by it? You stand still before it and your spirit leaps up in time with the waves.

That afternoon the sea was deep green jumpy and fog-shadowed. I was knotted tight with bad temper and my thoughts were so black they could have stained the inside of my head. I'd hoped by my absence to punish Joey. I'd forgotten he'd have Gracie for company. I tortured myself with visions of them sitting close and discussing war and World Events in slinky voices but a hundred yards on I was soon eased.

The sea did its business. It washed such thoughts away. Our troubles are nothing to it which is why watching it makes us so unmindful. The sea couldn't care less and that's how it should be.

I walked until evening and the fog had scattered to a mist that bleached the fields and turned the island into a pencil drawing waiting to be coloured in. The sea by now had grown flat as a spirit level and I was at a loss as to where I was and hungry not having eaten since breakfast. I kept on walking, Hitler happy at my heels, until something in the water caught my eye.

I looked down from a high rock and switched on my torch. Batteries were scarce so I only kept it on a few seconds at at a time. Later two fishermen would claim I'd been signalling the enemy. You see how the truth gets mangled.

At first I could see only the glitter my torch made on the waves then I became aware of a dark shape hardly thicker than a shadow moving below the surface and up it came, a seal. I'd never seen one all my years on the island although I'd often hoped. It rose bullet-headed out of the water silky moustache dripping black gobstopper eyes sad and peering up at me, looking not unlike Joseph Stalin after a bath. It ducked and dived all splash and foam like a sewing needle through layers of soft taffeta petticoats.

To see it seemed to me like a gift or benediction. Unworried and joyful it was at home in the sea and unbothered. I sat and watched it a full five minutes, my torch more on than off, a spotlight and the seal a dancer pleasing me the crowd.

The seal vanished and the day went with it. It was night but the sky was clear and fogless. There was a bomber's moon the colour of pearl but no sight for once of enemy planes, German or British. I walked on until I realised I was at the back of Ventnor and further from home than I'd have liked.

Joey would have left by now. Gracie would be on her own. I was resigned to her being there. I saw I had some duty to her. The seal could do as it liked. It lived in the sea which is kind and lets it be. On land life's different. There's always pressure and it's best to bend. I would go back to the Villa Judapah and knit Balaclavas. I'd write letters to Joey and be kind to Gracie Ballantyne. I'd have a good and quiet war. But not yet, I told myself, not yet. I'd stay here by the sea a little while longer.

I was at peace.

There was a cove close by I'd once found and had always meant to revisit. I thought to sit there undisturbed for a time but, wouldn't you know it, the army had been there already. They'd laced it over with barbed wire and had near to ruined it for me.

Now barbed wire's a nuisance but like nettles a confident hand will soon shift it. I cleared out a nice hollow for myself and a patch wide enough for the dog to run about although by now he was quite tired out.

The sand was blue in the moonlight and the dog so white he almost glowed. He was ever a dog to catch the light. The sea too was all a spangle. I took a paddle in it and sat on a rock to dry my feet. I kept the torch on to comfort the dog and relaxed.

I told myself this sorry affair of Joey the war and all else was just a dark cloud over the sun. It would soon pass. I didn't doubt it. I am an optimist. My mind is that way inclined. It works on an upward slope. It's hard-going sometimes but in the right direction. Content was how I was and close to dozing.

Then came trouble.

Two soldiers came upon me.

'Turn that fucking torch off!'

They were two black silhouettes high up on the cliff above. They came scrambling down in a cloud of falling rock and dust yelling their heads off at me.

The dog went berserk and I myself was in a panic with the noise of it all. I called him to heel and raised my hand to smack him but he barked on. I had to call and threaten him several times before he quietened to a growl.

'What you playing at?'

'Put out that fucking torch!'

'What you doing here?'

'I said, put out that fucking torch!'

'Come on, answer us, come on!'

They gave me no time to answer. They were so rude and aggressive fear made the words die in my throat. I couldn't hear to think my heart was banging so much.

I'd run up against soldiers before – more times than I've seen fit to mention – but that was in daylight. These two stood with the moon behind them black and solid taller than me and closer than I'd have liked. I could just make out their eyes, hard steely glints. Men in uniform have a way of looking at a woman makes her feel she's no more than a pair of legs in a skirt.

'What you doing here?'

'In the dark?'

'With that torch?'

'Come on, speak up!'

They had such heavy voices like each word had been dragged up out of their stomachs. One of them picked up my torch and shone it full in my face. I couldn't see for glare.

'Ay! What the hell is that?' he said and dropped the torch.

'Jesus!' said the other and the pair of them stood back.

I couldn't understand why but something had changed. They were as afraid of me as I had been of them.

One of them, the younger one, bent down for the torch. He shone it full at me again. His voice was softer now. He pointed at my shoulder and asked in all seriousness and wonder, 'Are you a spy?'

I looked down to where he'd pointed. There on my lapel was a tiny swastika.

Believe me, this is how it happened. I'd left the house in a rage, as you know. I'd flounced out grabbing my coat my bag and the lead. By the coatstand was that *Daily Express* Map of the War with its little stickers forever falling out. One had caught in my hair. I'd found it there when watching the seal. I'd stuck it in my lapel for safekeeping. I did it without even looking.

It was being looked at now. These two soldiers, they were such gawps. I was no longer frightened.

'You're a spy, aren't you?'

The devil was in me and I said, 'Oh, yes, we spies always walk about with swastikas attached.'

I'd long had the feeling that the army weren't sending their best men to the island. We can't have been a priority even though Germany was only a few miles across the Channel. These two looked as if they'd struggle counting to twenty even with their socks off. I decided to string them along. It was only a bit of fun and who's averse to that?

'Hitler and me are best friends,' I said. I was stroking

the dog as I said it. I was as good as pointing at it. I was giving them every chance. They must have known the dog's name. They'd heard me calling it to heel.

'Shut up!' said the younger one all nervy. He meant it as an order but it sounded like he was begging.

The other one, the older one, was meaner. He had a pistol with him. He took it out slipped the catch pulled the trigger and aimed it at me. I'd not seen a pistol before or not up close. I wasn't scared. He wouldn't have shot me. If he tried, he'd have missed.

'You're coming with us. Get up!'

I did get up but I wasn't going anywhere but home. I thought of Gracie alone in the house.

'Look, lads, I'm in a rush. And you two must be busy, what with having an island to defend. I don't live far. My name's Mabel Daley Bancroft. I live at the Villa Judapah. I've got someone staying. Her husband's been dead two days so I must get back. Here's ten shillings. Go buy yourself some fags.'

A ten bob note could get you two hundred cigarettes. I'd not meant to be so generous only I'd no small change.

'What you trying to do? Bribe us, you Nazi cow?'

'Walk, you bitch, hands high!'

I had no choice. I clambered up the cliff path and walked all the way to their camp with my hands up and cursing them not always under my breath. My arms burned with aching. It's never pleasant to walk in the dark with two men behind you, one with a gun and both of them muttering comments on your body as if it's a thing they own and don't much like.

The dog followed, confused.

Coming into camp the pair acted as if they'd caught the whole German army. They called out to their mates they'd captured a dangerous Fifth Columnist. One or two recognised me and laughed.

'You've got Crazy Mabel there. She lives in that mad pagoda on the chine. She's no spy. She's harmless.'

'Oh yeah?' said my captors. 'Well, she's a fucking German agent and we've got proof.'

I suppose they meant my swastika which proved nothing other than I read the *Daily Express* which I didn't so what kind of proof was that? Some people, you give them brains wrapped up in a parcel they'd not be able to untie the string.

I was put in an office and left alone with a phone a filing cabinet and a snowdrift of paperwork on the desk. Not very bright of them if I had been a spy. I took a bundle of letters and such things and put them in my bag.

I wasn't kept waiting long. An officer not quite in uniform – no tie and a pair of slippers – came in and interviewed me.

'I am Mabel Daley Bancroft,' I said not for the first time. 'I live at the Villa Judapah. I'm no more a spy than this dog. 'If I was, would I be walking around with a swastika on my coat?'

'No, you wouldn't, Mrs Bancroft. Would you like a mint? I've a lady friend who makes them. Of course, with the war on, she uses honey, not sugar, but I think they're jolly fine all the same. What do you think?'

Like lamb's vomit I thought but I didn't say. This man was at least polite despite having grey nails. I gave the mint to the dog who ate it readily enough. I imagine it tasted better than the telephone wire he'd been chewing.

'I'm sorry,' I explained, 'mint's not a favourite of mine. It puts me in mind of sheep and them I've never liked. They look at you all blank and unknowing but who's to say what goes on in their heads. At the VJ I'll boil mutton and I'll roast lamb but I'll not partake myself. That said, I'm as fond of woollen goods as anybody.'

'Quite. Speaking of wool, you certainly pulled some over two of my men's eyes tonight.'

'Well, they're not the greatest of brains, are they?'

'They are a little raw, yes. And edgy. We all are. The

Jerries are only a few miles away. We've only the Channel between us. Everyone is a little tense.'

'The Germans won't come!' I said it as if I knew it for a fact. He looked interested but pressed on.

'The fact is, Mrs Bancroft . . . Can I call you Mabel?'

'Call me what you like.'

'The fact is, Mabel, lovey, you've been very silly. Your name is already known to me. If I could find it in that cabinet, there's a file on you. You've been reported several times and had some very harsh warnings about being laggardly with your blackout. We've been a naughty girl, haven't we, Mabel? I don't think you appreciate what a knife-edge situation this is. And pretending to be a Fifth Columnist! Not terribly clever, are we? Such people do exist. They are a real threat. They are the Trojan Horse within our walls and may cost us the war. You don't want nasty German chappies staying rent-free at the Villa Judas?'

'Judapah!' I corrected him. The man was a fool and worse he thought I was one too.

'Carry on as you have been doing, my girl, and somebody may take you for a spy. That would mean prison. It might even mean a hangman's noose. You'd better watch your step, young Mabel.'

I could have said something but I'd not eaten since breakfast. I decided to be contrite.

'This doesn't have to be a military matter. I'm going to ask the police to deal with you. They've little enough to do. If you're lucky, you'll just get off with another warning but I'd advice you to think on, young lady, think on.'

'Can I go now?'

'Yes, but wait one moment.'

He left. The dog had made a mess of the telephone wire. It was badly frayed and there was nothing else for it but to cut it clean with the paper knife.

'Bad dog!'

I tidied the wires under the mat.

I thought the officer had gone to get me a car but no he came back and said, 'Righto, you can go now. Don't come back.'

I had to walk.

The moon was still up but day was breaking the sky mauve edged with gold. The sea was silver. What a day and a night I'd had! I was dizzy with the way the world turns creakily slowly then in jolts and bounds. I'd been miserable and then a thing had happened which had made me laugh. There was a click as of a jigsaw fitting into place. I felt complete but too tired to think why.

Going home I was very Scarlett O'Hara. Tomorrow I'll think about it tomorrow. I needed sleep and a good breakfast.

The VJ was pink in the early light but inside the house was dark. Gracie was asleep but the cooker was warm. Four ounces of bacon and two eggs had gone from the larder. She'd helped herself. She may have been made a widow but she'd not changed her scavenging ways.

It was an affair of fuss and no consequence. Once I'd recovered my good temper I found I couldn't care less. I allowed myself to think no more of their bad manners and allegations. Much of the next day passed without a word of it soiling my mind.

Gracie was quiet too. There was the occasional sniff and gulping back of tears. I could hardly hold this against her although I prefer other people's grief dry-eyed and silent – there's less phlegm involved.

Evening found her in the parlour with me. The light was dim and outside was damp. I suppose it reminded her of her husband.

'It's hard to credit he's only been dead three days,' I said by way of sympathy.

'These are terrible times,' she said. She'd lost weight and looked haggard. She'd never look faintly young again. 'Nothing seems real to me. Nothing is certain. A building is there one moment, gone the next. You have a husband. You spend your life by his side. You become a widow in a second and must learn to speak of him in the past tense. It's all too frightful. If the world ends, it will end like this, the work of a moment.'

'The world won't end,' I said. 'It's not in its nature to end.'

What I said was true – I've yet to be proved wrong – but she wasn't to be consoled.

'Nothing is to be trusted. You can't even be sure that one second will follow another without your whole life changing horribly in the interval. Oh, Mabel, it's all so beastly and unfair.'

I decided this an avenue of thought she could travel down alone. I turned on the wireless for the German news. I thought a bit of Lord Haw-Haw would cheer me up.

At the very sound of him Gracie rose up all fiery out of her gloom.

'Mabel! That's William Joyce! The man's a traitor. Turn it off. Turn it off! Have you no thought for me at all. Men like him killed my husband. Turn it off. His voice sickens me.'

'Well, come to that, I'm not too fond of your voice either but I've had to sit here listening to you chunter on. Besides it is my wireless. I think he's got a lovely voice, mellow. The dog likes it.'

The dog was at my feet paddling his legs in some doggy dream. It couldn't be called upon to give evidence but our spat came to nothing. The doorbell rang. The dog shot up barking.

Despite claiming all that day to have been 'quite paralysed with misery' Gracie ran to the door as if it were her own to open. I heard her say, 'Do come in, Constable, this way.' I turned down Lord Haw-Haw to a burble.

Gracie entered the policeman following. She thought he'd come to arrest us for listening to the German news. It may well have been an offence.

I'd seen him before on his rounds but we'd never spoken. He was a hairy individual, curly and red. It crept up over his collar and cuffs and made it seem as if his neck and wrists were fraying.

'Mrs Bancroft? Mabel Bancroft?'

'The one and only. Sit down. You're too tall to be on your feet. We've just been listening to Lord Haw-Haw.'

Gracie paled and looked set to join her husband at this confession. I hoped she'd go and give us privacy but she was without manners.

'Really?' said the constable. 'I listen to him myself now and then. He's often right.'

'I imagine he's in close contact with his Führer. I expect they pass in the corridor and Adolf tells him the news.'

'I wouldn't be too surprised at that, Mrs Bancroft. He must get his information from somewhere.'

It was as I'd thought – the man was stupid. The clever men (if any there are) were gone away and somewhere else. This one, not content with hairy wrists and neck, was growing a ginger fuzz to cover his drooping lips. I suppose it gave him a hobby now that he had bitten his nails ragged.

'I'd have come sooner. I've had you on my list since breakfast but I've been waylaid.'

'You're here now anyway.'

'Yes, I am. I'm here now, yes.'

He didn't sound too sure.

'Well, that's nice for all concerned,' I said.

'There was a bit of a to-do.'

'Was there?'

'At Ventnor. We found a German. Or a farmer did. In his barn.'

'No!' said Gracie. 'A German!'

'Yes, a German.'

'A real German? Gosh!'

'Yes,' I said losing patience, 'a real German. As opposed to these imitation Germans we see about us every day. He wasn't wearing a little swastika, was he?'

'He was in uniform, Mrs Bancroft. That's how we could tell. The Home Guard marched him into Shanklin. I've had him under lock and key all day until a boat was found to take him to the mainland. He came down in a plane. It crashed in the sea.'

'He must have swum to the shore,' said Gracie ever the great mind.

'He might have walked on the water?' I said and watched them both entertain this possibility.

'He was only young but he wasn't a bit sorry he was German. They breed them vicious there.'

My heart went out to the German boy. I imagined him nervous and pimply yelled and prodded at as he was marched across the fields. I'd had an experience not unlike it.

'Poor lamb,' I said almost aloud.

'No, it was chickens,' said the policeman.

'What was chickens?'

'The farmer who found him. He had chickens, not lambs.'

'That must be nice for him,' I said. How else could I answer?

He turned to Gracie.

'Are you a resident here, Mrs . . .'

'Ballantyne,' I answered for her. 'She's a guest really but her husband fiddled some forms early on. He's dead now. It's been three days, hasn't it? His body might arrive any moment. She's still quite upset, aren't you?'

Gracie said yes and bit her lip. Her eyes were silvery with tears but not one of them fell. The constable gave his condolences.

'Gracie love,' I said sweetly, 'this gentleman and I have things to discuss. Do you mind removing yourself, pray?'

Reluctantly she went. She left the door ever so slightly ajar. I've no doubt she was knees down with her ear jammed against the crack for a good earwig. I didn't blame her. I'd have done the same.

'Well, Mrs Bancroft, we've been having some trouble with you and that's no lie.'

He talked to me as though I was six. It's a habit men have. I replied all girlish, 'Me?' Shirley Temple could have taken lessons. I even had a thumb in my mouth.

'Trespass, 31 July,' he said flicking through his notebook. I say 'flick' but it was more of a slow trudge. 'Shifting barbed wire . . . 5 August . . . seen arguing with soldiers . . . Culver Down . . . 7 August trespass . . . Sandown beach . . . Shanklin beach . . . 10 August trespass . . . 11 August . . . endeavouring to force a seaguard . . . 12 August . . .'

I'd been busy. It sounded worse piled up in a list but each event had been minor enough in itself. I'd be out with the dog strolling where I wasn't supposed to stroll. Some soldier would yell at me to move on. I'd yell back and move on eventually. I'd not thought somebody'd be taking notes. I thought with a war on they'd have better things to do.

The constable droned on until he reached the events of the night before. No word was said about the papers I'd stolen or the telephone wire but it seems I'd been found sitting under a concealed coastal gun.

'How was I supposed to know that if it was concealed?'

'All the same, this can't go on. This here is a whole catalogue of misdemeanours and blind eyes can be turned no more. Take last night, you were seen flashing a torch.'

'Oh, I was just signalling the enemy. There's a submarine pops up quite often. I was flashing at them for five minutes but they didn't show. These Germans, they're not reliable.'

An intelligent man at this point might have rumbled me but the Great Detective just pulled out his pencil licked it and said, 'Go on, I'm listening.'

'Go on what? Why?'

'Anything. I'm listening. My pencil is poised.'

'What else do you want to know?'

He thought for a second then asked me if it was true that last night I'd conducted a one woman storm rally.

It took me a while to understand. Then I realised. It was when I was calling the dog to heel. I daresay it could sound like Heil Hitler to anyone with deficient hearing and a malicious mind.

'Yes,' I said, 'I was. I also goosestep occasionally. Excellent exercise. Really trims the tum. You should try it.'

He wrote this down.

'Do I take it then that you are a supporter of the German army?'

This was as direct a question as I could expect. I answered it plainly.

'No, but I'm very fond of Hitler.' I reached down and let the dog lick my hand. 'He's a regular pet.'

This also went down in his notebook.

'Do you not think, Mrs Bancroft, that such opinions are irresponsible in a time of war?'

I felt as if I was being interviewed on the Home Service. I'd had enough.

'War? I'm sick of it. It's time we blew the whistle and went home. I've a business on its knees and a dog I've nowhere to walk. I've black paint on my windows with no notion how to scrape it off should peace ever come which I doubt, some folk love this war so much. Let the Germans come. Let the Italians come. Let them all come. The Germans aren't so bad. They're only taking land and we've done plenty of that in the past. Look at the globe. Bits of pink everywhere and we're the tiniest blob of all but we rule over the whole lot. We've more than our fair share.

I can't bring myself to blame the Germans for wanting likewise.'

The constable wrote this down too. He stuck his tongue out as he did so. He said it helped him think. He needed something.

'Is that why you listen to Lord Haw-Haw?'

'I don't listen to him. The dog does.'

'You know he doesn't tell the truth?'

'What, the dog?'

'No, Lord Haw-Haw. Not all of it. Sometimes none of it.'

'Truth? Who cares for that? They say it's war's first casualty but so what? I've never seen anybody weep for it. I don't see those who govern us raising the alarm and saying "Oh, look, truth's been wounded. Oh dear, let's make up and be friends again." It just makes them fight meaner. And if truth's so easily hurt, what good is it?'

Gracie came back in. How much she heard I can't say and care less. What could either of them do? I had opinions of my own. Is that a crime?

'We'll be in touch, Mrs Bancroft. I'd advise you to mend your ways.'

I didn't like his tone. I said, 'This lady's husband's dead in the Blitz. A house fell on him. My Joey's off fighting fires. You come here bothering poor women who just want to be left alone. Does that make you proud? Is that good war work? Why aren't you in the army killing Germans?'

'Because I'm in a reserved occupation, I'm thirty-four and have bad asthma,' he answered me flatly.

That put me in my place.

We had another air raid that night. The first bomb fell on Shanklin. It hit Napier House on the Esplanade. After the raid a soldier was sent to a hotel further up to tell some refugees it was safe to come out. He went to Napier House by mistake. It was still standing and looked untouched. He rang the doorbell and the whole building came crashing down about him. He wasn't hurt just dusty saved by the porch the only bit left standing.

I never saw much of the air raids. The worst came after me. That night I spent under the table with Gracie squeezing the life out of my legs she was that scared. I wondered how she'd been any good in the Blitz. Later she fell asleep. I tried to shift her and as she rolled over she murmured her dead husband's name to herself. If I'd been so disturbed would I have muttered Joey? It's not a thing I'll ever know.

It was Gracie who found out about Napier House. One of the soldiers in the next field told her. I was signing a telegram that said Ayres Ballantyne had turned up in Ryde.

He came in a sealed box and we buried him in it. I paid for the service so it was quite cheap. Gracie said she'd pay me back. I said I'd not hold my breath.

Joey didn't come. He was fighting fires on the Isle of Dogs. I questioned his sense of priorities.

That night we opened a bottle of port. Drink makes me tender. I let Gracie open her heart. It turns out I was right. They'd never been married.

'It was something other people did. We thought we were special, you see, unique. It was pompous of us really. Besides, Ayres had been married before, a dreadful woman who danced for money or so I'm told. It didn't matter. We were drifters. In younger, happier days we went everywhere. Persia. Alexandria. Kenya. Such adventures we had. Such thrilling times. We didn't have a home. The VJ was the nearest we ever came to it. You and Joey seemed to us so solid, so tremendously, you know, real. We thought of you as family. It was all we asked. A room, a table, a good bed and some chairs. Little enough to ask and yet it's gone in a moment.'

I was touched. It may have been the port. I might have squeezed her hand for company's sake but I had a pencil and paper in mine.

'When I first knew Ayres I longed to be away from him. Our love was so intense. I would wish he wasn't there so I could dream of him. Is that too silly of me, do you think?'

'Well, you've got your wish now.'

I meant it kindly enough but she cried. After a bit she stopped snivelling.

'What are you doing?'

'Oh, this?' I said putting it away in a drawer. 'It's nothing. Top secret. Can't tell you.'

I was drawing maps. I'd been doing them since the constable left. I was remembering walks I'd taken the dog. I was imagining floating up and looking down on the island tracing its waving coastline.

I doubt my maps were accurate. I doubt they were more than doodles. My head was filled with soft ideas.

I thought, if I was a spy how would I see this island? Where would I tell the Germans to land? Where would I tell them to aim their bombs? Who would I tell them to capture? I thought of the sweetbreads Brewer kept under the counter and never thought of giving me. I thought of Alicia who still did my hair but who stinted on lacquer and was rough with the comb. I thought of the policeman and of Miss Ithell at the library who sneezed on your books and then wiped them with her sleeve. I made a list of these and others under the heading 'Those To Be Attended To.'

I did it all quite idly and to pass the time.

Honestly.

I was no more for the Germans than I was against them but I quite liked the idea of being a spy.

I'd say the word to myself in the mirror. If I stood in front of it and said Mabel Daley Bancroft it never felt right. The reflection it disowned me. 'Spy,' I'd say softly and then I'd laugh. I'd laugh not because it was funny but because it was possible.

Monday morning five days after the visit from PC Plod there was a summons on the mat. I was to appear in court for trespass and offering bribes to soldiers.

'Oh, Mabel! cried Gracie, reading over my shoulder.

'Spy,' I said very softly but loud enough for her to hear. Then I laughed.

4

I woke before sunrise restless. I padded about the house went extravagant lit a fire fed the dog and sat watching him eat.

I was acting as if at a loss but I wasn't.

I've never claimed my mind's an arrow. It's never flown straight. It goes where it likes and I'm surprised at the notions it hits on. This said, I've never held wrong thoughts by accident. I knew what I was about to do was wrong but it didn't feel it. It felt comfortable.

Idly idly as if dreaming but knowing really knowing I took my ID card out of the tea caddy and carefully erased my name with a rubber band. They were cheap tatty things that smudged soon as look at them. With my good pen I printed a new name and number.

The number I no longer remember but my new name came on me like the Holy Ghost. Gretta Pollack. Gretta had been Mother's name and as foreign in sound as I dared get. Pollack came from my being such a fan of their lilac floor wax. There'd been a tin of it on the table at the time.

Careful though I had been, I did make one mistake. I rested my hand while writing 'Pollack' and made a full stop. As a consequence I was to be called Gretta P. Ollack.

After a giggle, I didn't much mind. It had an alien ring. It wasn't ideal for a spy passing herself off as British but I didn't want to be too subtle.

In fact I didn't want to be subtle at all.

I did likewise with my ration book after dropping it in water sponging off the ink and pressing it dry with a middle to warm iron. It took an age.

Gracie came down for breakfast and I hid the papers under the tablecloth. She'd been looking at me strange since the summons. She was persuading me to see a doctor. She said a court might look kindly on a sick note for stress brought on by war.

'There's still time if you go this morning. You're not due at court until this afternoon, are you?'

The post came and changed the subject.

The subject it changed to was Joey. He'd written to Gracie with money to spend on flowers for the grave.

'He sends his love,' she lied.

I thought the money should have gone on paying her keep but another idea had come to me.

'Don't get flowers, get plants. Plants last longer. They're more economic.'

This appealed to her.

'Why not go into Ryde? You'll have far more choice there. Go today.'

'But I was thinking of going to court with you.'

'I don't need company for that. Go on, have a day out. It'll do you good. Take the whole day.'

I began packing the moment she left. I took no clothes of my own but the best of hers. I never had a dress that didn't sag on me as if being worn was too much work for it. Her clothes had weighted hems ribbed bodices and stiffened bustards. They were like armour and I was going into battle.

They were a bugger to fold into a tiny suitcase. They kept springing out standing up and accusing me of their kidnapping. I also took three hats but ones that squashed and took up less space like the *diamanté* cap she'd worn that first night at the VJ.

Now I Mabel Daley Bancroft cared nothing for hats – they cost too much and make your head sweat. Dresswise I kept to basic black with aprons my one extravagance and the odd good blouse. This is how it should be for such as me. Too entrancing an appearance takes a guest's mind off his food. The finer effects of your cooking go unnoticed. Decorate the plate and not the body is this landlady's motto but Gretta P. Ollack was no landlady. She was a peacock. She liked to be seen. Only in death safe in a coffin would her legs have gone without stockings or her face without powder. She was also unmarried. I left my wedding ring in the tea caddy and gave Joey not a thought as I did so.

Amazing how much I knew about her. It was as if the decision to be another person was enough to bring that person to life.

I also packed the wireless. It was walnut-cased a foot long and six inches deep. I could have done without it but who ever heard of a spy without a radio?

I had as good a lunch as possible on a whole week's rations – Gracie could fend for herself – and stood buttoned up and ready to go. I was in the hall and might have looked about me longer had I realised then it would be the last I'd see of the VJ for many years.

It was the dining room that caught me. It was shadowed in blackout but once my red velvet curtains had hung there. In summer the sun would pour through them and the room looked soaked in wine. I took them out of the airing cupboard and wrapped them round the wireless. I suppose I wanted a memento. Guests steal soap on the same principle. I should have taken something smaller like an ashtray but I don't smoke.

Packing and parcelling had not been the only occupation of the morning. Most of it had been spent making a mess. I'd strewn the rooms with maps and coded messages I'd devised as well as the papers I'd stolen the night the soldiers had caught me. I ransacked the drawers and pulled off all the sheets but my best lark was painting a huge swastika in red on the hall. I'd never been fond of that wallpaper and now the swastika made decorating a must. It would give me something to do when I got back.

I took one last confidence-building look in the mirror at Gretta P. Ollack and left. As I closed the door I heard Hitler in the bathroom whining for food and company. Gracie could give him both.

It was midday and shadowless the sky ash-blue hazy with heat, not a day to be travelling with my little load. The soldier in the next field watched me go. He took an uncommon interest in my luggage but made no effort to help me with it.

I caught the bus outside the grocer's. He saw me through the window. We'd rowed the day before over some potatoes. They'd been spotted black right through. War's no excuse for bad vegetables, I'd said. I'd also left a coded note in the VJ instructions to the Germans when they landed to capture the greengrocer first and force feed him with his own sprouts.

The bus pulled up and I got on. I settled my bags and went to the driver.

'Freshwater, a single, please.'

I knew the driver by sight. He was the brother of Molly or Dolly but he was without a cleft palate and bore no ill feeling. He had hands cleaner than is normal in a bus driver but a hole in the heart kept him from fighting Germans. He gave me my ticket and I said, *'Danke schön,'* to my surprise and his. I knew no German but it seems Gretta Ollack did. She had a nerve displaying her flair for languages with the enemy so near. People were on the look-out for them. Who was to say that the first to arrive wasn't going to be a lady in a hat and too much hand luggage?

I went back to my seat and saw him look at me in his rear-view mirror. He muttered something to the passenger behind him who also turned and looked. It may have been about nuns with hairy hands. I took off a glove and fanned my face. They could see my hand was quite bald. They seemed content with this and we gave each other no further thought.

The bus changed at Ventnor. It gave me an hour to spend at the Air and Angels Café, a bijou place too good for the riff-raff who normally come to Ventnor. I had a very moist scone and tea in a china cup. Pleased with such a treat, under the saucer I left a shilling tip and a swastika.

The ride from Ventnor to Freshwater I don't recommend even now. This island was never meant for traffic. The roads are narrow and nothing but curves. We got stuck behind a horse and watercart sprinkling the roads to keep the dust down and then we stopped behind a cow with mastitis.

I just relaxed. A spy like me should have been making plans but I lost myself in the view of soft fields and glittering sea. What thoughts I did have were of Miss Ollack and of Mother.

No one knew better than me that there was no Gretta Ollack yet here she was in clothes she'd chosen herself and exhibiting a free and easy style that was different in kind from my own heavy way of doing things. I realised that we were the same person. I had made her up. She was a lie made real and that's what called to mind my mother.

Mother had re-imagined herself. Stuck in Cheamish with Father and alone too long with Miss Bird, lies had released her. They'd given her dull life pep. Lies do that. All sorts is possible. They don't govern the world but kaleidoscope it. Like Presto they create magic.

Mother had known this. Such knowledge was my legacy and I had finally come of age. I dedicated my adventure to her.

There's not much to Freshwater a pleasing bay a bit of shingle a few boats bobbing about and a smell of fish. It has a charm and historic echo owing to Lord Tennyson having lived there encouraging famous visitors in his lifetime and the more sensitive day-tripper since his death. A historic figure is good for trade. Sandown has need of one. Vainly I used to think in time I might be that figure with my statue in the High Street but I'm forgotten and unknown which is why I did what I did and now write it all down here so that someone will take note I lived a less than ordinary life.

The driver helped me out with my bags and I gave him a threepenny bit tip.

'Thanks very much, Mrs B.'

'*Danke schön,*' I said in turn.

He laughed but not readily. I felt him watch me as I walked off, not a pleasant sensation to be watched from behind but one to be suffered. Why else was I doing this if not to be watched?

I sat awhile by the sea to get my bearings. Up on the redoubt there were two soldiers on guard. They were eating Spam butties and paid me no mind when I walked past. I thought it best not to bother them. Not having turned up for court that afternoon Mabel Daley Bancroft was now a wanted woman.

I had tea at Claribel's and another at the Moated Grange which also did meringues – dried egg and bicarb (war drives people to such crimes). I whiled my afternoon away with a pad and pencil noting the number of people coming out of the chemist's and writing in code a quick description of each. I thought it a thing a spy might do. I left swastikas under the saucers of nearby tables and notes saying 'Hitler lands tonight'. I was sad to go before these were found. In my head I often imagine the panic they might have caused.

I picked out a little B&B called, with no regard for geography, Loch Lomond. A cramped dwelling it had a view of the sea and the redoubt above the bay. Mrs McLelland was already at the door wiping down her vacancies sign. She seemed glad of a guest. She gave off a smell of the bacon her regular clientele no doubt stole from her break-fast table and kept in their pockets for lunch.

I said, 'I am Miss Ollack. Gretta P. Here is my ID card. I am a teacher of young girls in Ryde. I have come to Freshwater for a few days' rest. Have you a room in which I may reside?'

I spoke very slowly and with care to give the effect of English being as familiar in my mouth as a pebble. Mrs McLelland took my voice to be not foreign but posh. She decided poor woman to compete and invented some airs for herself. I do find it sad when folk do this.

'Oh, I shall be delighted to have you abode here, Miss Ollack was it?'

She was cursed with a sing-song voice. Whatever she set out to say would always end on a high note. She wasn't a person you'd want at a funeral.

'I am most obliged to have you patronise me, Miss Ollack. A single or a double, is it? Have a double why not I've loads of room. Come walk this way.'

She trudged back into the house. It was as I imagined. She drew her guests from the working class. The bright orange hall had never known wallpaper and she had lino on the floor. I made no comment. I looked kindly on her and did not condemn her out of hand for her poor taste and low standards.

'Perhaps, Miss Ollack, before I conduce you to your room I might lead you along the vestibule so you may witness what I like to call my conservatoiree.'

I had a strong idea that Mrs McLelland showed all her guests the conservatory first. It was to make up for the dingy bedroom she'd show them next.

'My son put up the conservatoiree the year before the war. It has provoked innumerate compliments and is quite a talking point with all my guests.'

Her 'conservatoiree' was a shabby affair, no more than a greenhouse with a few deck chairs flung in. I saw cracked glass and bird business and each pane had been covered with brown paper for the blackout which rather defeated the exercise.

'Very nice,' I said. 'Like Crystal Palace,' I added meaning that like Crystal Palace it ought to have been burned down.

'It's here my guests like to congeal of an evening. I did have an idea for some exotic plants in here but they didn't thrive. Those are potatoes growing in the corner. My bit for the war effort. We must all do something must not we, Miss Ollack?'

'Quite,' I said peaceably.

There was a poster 'Careless Talk Cost Lives' pinned up in the hallway and from the kitchen I could hear Alvar Liddell mumbling the news. Mrs M. was one of those who made a hobby of following the war.

'Ollack? That's not a name one hears every day.'

'Yes, it does have a faintly foreign sound to it, does it not?'

At this she gave me a look. 'Is it foreign by any chance pray?'

'It may well be. I've met a few people on the Continent with the same name.'

'Go abroad much do we, Miss Ollack?' Her eyes narrowed.

'It's like a second home. Have you ever been abroad?'

'I have not!' she said defiantly but I gave her such a pitying look she feared she'd slipped too far down the social scale than was safe and so she added, 'I have been to Isle of Mull. You have to go across in a boat. Does that count as abroad?'

'It might pass,' I said generously.

'Perhaps after this present crisis I might partake of European air.'

I doubted it and so did she.

'This present crisis will retreat,' I said rolling my r's to sound more foreign but ending up closer to Glasgow. 'Mr Hitler is only just across the Channel.'

'Well, let's hope it does soon but with him a little further away than that.'

I said nothing. She heard me say nothing.

'Perhaps, Miss Ollack, we will see you in the conservatoiree after dinner which is at seven sharp. I have few guests at the moment but Mrs Gobowen of Sea Idyll often pops by. We imbibe of port and lemon together very civilised I think you'll find. I say port and lemon but it's really sherry and lemon substitute. This war's harsh on citrus as you may know, Miss Ollack.'

She did so love saying that name. She seemed to be testing it with her tongue to see if it'd break.

'Why, Mrs McFadden, that is most inviting of you.'

'It's McLelland, not McFadden.'

'Is it? Such a quaint name. Is it Welsh?'

It wasn't a pleasant room I was given narrow dark with a bed by the window because there was nowhere else it would go. There were no flowers only a vase cracked with a green scum on the bottom. The rug was crusty with toenails and the candlewick bedspread had been picked bald by previous guests no doubt during the sleepless nights spent on a mattress so thin it could have been folded four times over and still only made a very flat pillow. How unlike my dear VJ.

I unwrapped the wireless first. Mrs M. had commented

on my wealth of luggage and had asked me what was the thing in red velvet.

'It's awful heavy,' she said picking it up.

'Put that down!' I snapped.

She dropped it with such a clunk it embarrassed us both.

'What have you in there, Miss Ollack, pray?' she'd asked. 'Bricks?'

I'd told her they were only nick-nacks to remind me of my fatherland.

Despite its fall it was unharmed. I put it in the wardrobe tuned to a station that was all fizz and static. I muffled it further with the candlewick bedspread. With the door closed it was but a faint sound as of mice tap-dancing. There was though a definite smell of mice in Loch Lomond and a danger of Mrs M. not noticing. Tap-dancing mice might have been an everyday event for her so I turned it up a fraction more. An odd word or two was audible. It was not unlike sharing a room with a companionable ghost. I recommend this tactic to the lonely.

From my window I could see only the top of the redoubt and so I drew my maps from memory. I was not convinced of its strategic importance. Its bay was too small for battle-ships and the coast too rocky for landings but I did make a note of the shops with two black marks against the Moated Grange. The service had been slow and the wait-ress I'd swear had eczema.

I also wrote out a list of made-up names in a code of my own devising. It was hardly an enigma and would take only a second to work out but it looked like a code which is what matters.

I put a couple of maps and messages in a drawer and left a few scrumpled up in the wicker wastebasket. If Mrs M. was a landlady through to her bones and not by acci-dent she'd soon sniff them out.

*

'I was just passing your room, Miss Ollack,' she said when I came down for dinner at seven sharp, 'and I had such a turn. I thought I was hearing voices but I expect you're like me, I'm always talking to myself.'

'First sign of madness,' I said.

We laughed.

'You go ahead into the dining arena, Miss Ollack. I'll be serving up in a mo'. Just want to slip my teeth in. All right?'

The dining arena was a puce room with a table. There was no serving trolley and not even a sideboard for condiments. Mrs M. carried in the food on a tray with a dent in it.

'A woman came from the WI on a tin drive. She said can we have that tray and I said no you can't the cheek! I know each scratch in it and it's old enough to be valuable. You won't desist from the soup will you, Miss Ollack?'

She smiled to show off her dentures.

'Pass Miss Ollack the bread basquette, Mr Oates, there's a kindness.'

Mr Oates his pale wife and child were her only other guests and they'd be gone in the morning.

'Mr and Mrs Oates are from Poole in Dorset and this is their little Jamie who is quite the spit of his father think not you, Miss Ollack? Mr Oates is a chartered surveyor which is a preserved occupation in case you're wondering why he's not in the army like other innumerate young men. You don't mind me thus explaining, Mr O.?'

Mr Oates shrugged his shoulders but I saw his lip quiver. A man not dressed for war is always touchy on the subject. I smiled to signify I cared not a fig what he was wearing.

'Miss Ollack is a teacher, Young Jamie, so you mind your manners. Oh he's a lovely lump isn't he, Miss Ollack, couldn't you just eat him up?'

Young Jamie was a sullen six-year-old. He was picking his nose and watching it float on the soup.

'We're here for a wedding,' said Mrs Oates. When she spoke she had a vague look of someone not listening to her own words but to an invisible orchestra playing just above her head. 'It's my sister's wedding. We were split at birth.'

'Oh dear.'

'Our mother wasn't a well woman. We were based in Leatherhead. Father sold furniture. That meant a lot of moving about. We had an aunty in Leicester so we kept in touch. I was sixteen before I met Shirley again but I could have picked her out in a queue. Isn't that strange?'

'She doesn't want to hear all this, Naomi,' her husband snapped – as far as anyone can snap a name like Naomi. 'Jamie, drink that soup!'

Jamie said he couldn't. There were nose droppings in it.

'No, there isn't, that's parsley. Now drink it!'

'Is your sister marrying an army man?' I asked.

'I suppose she must be. He wears a uniform. He's called Lenny which is a name new to me but I believe it's quite common. He comes from Halifax and that must explain it.'

'Is he based on the island? At Ventnor? There's a radar station in Ventnor.'

'No, he's very much on his own at Brighstone. He says he doesn't mind and quite likes the company. He's not a man I'd marry. The reception's at Brighstone although what reception can you have with rations the way they are? I've a trifle upstairs.'

'Very much on his own? At Brighstone? What can he be doing there?'

'Naomi!' butted in Mr Oates. He made it sound like a burp.

'It's something to do with the post or so he says. The mail's not very reliable these days. I don't suppose that's his fault though.'

'Naomi!' Mr Oates warned her again.

She ignored him as she ignored Young Jamie playing submarines with the salt cellar.

'I think he intercepts the mail. He has stamps from all over. He showed us one last night from the Bahamas. You wouldn't think a place so small would have a stamp but the Isle of Man has one so who's to say?'

'And who'd be writing from the Bahamas in a time of war? That is intriguing. Did Lenny say?'

It's easy being a spy when your enemies are folk like Naomi.

'I wouldn't know but I was reading in *The People's Friend* how the Duke of Windsor is going to live there. I was sad to see him go although I'll not have a word said against the Queen. The Princess Margaret Rose is a lovely child. They say she's as tall as our Jamie. Lenny didn't say if the stamp came from the Duke of Windsor, did he, Leslie. You'd think he would with us being nearly family.'

'I think you've said enough for the time being. Lenny showed us that in strictest confidence. It's not a thing to be divulged. I'm sorry, Miss Ollack, but careless talk costs lives. And it wasn't the Bahamas, it was Fiji.'

Mrs M. took our soup bowls away and came back with rissoles. I didn't ask for the recipe. I let things slide as we chewed over our dinner but it was hard to resist.

'Fiji? What part are they playing in this war?'

'You're not asking me, are you? I wouldn't know Fiji if I stood on it.'

'But this Lenny must have said something surely?'

The husband came in again.

'I think you've asked enough. I'm sorry to be rude but much of this war is very hush-hush and not for the dinner table.'

'But we're only talking, Leslie.'

'There were people who thought they were "only talking" to Mata Hari. Do we know this woman. Who are you?'

'She's Miss Ollack. We've been introduced. You are

being rude and I know why. It's because I spent too much on Shirley's present. You know I was only making up for all those lost years. Anyway, this lady's not German, look how she holds her knife and fork.'

'With a name like Ollack she can't be normal.'

'Leslie! I do apologise. He's been like this since I showed him that present. It's a fan made of slate.'

'How nice,' I said. 'That'll be useful in hot weather.'

'And in winter they can keep it on the mantelpiece. See, Leslie, does she sound German?'

'She doesn't need to sound German. Last week in the *Express* there was an enemy agent travelled from Dover to London by train. Perfect English. A bus conductor caught him. Didn't understand what a one and threepenny was. Imagine the damage if he'd got as far as Downing Street.'

Jamie began to cry. Faced with Mrs M.'s cooking I'd say it was a reasonable response.

'I am sorry. He was evacuated to Pwllheli. It was only for a fortnight but they spoke Welsh at him. He's been upset ever since.'

'The poor lamb,' I said, 'pass him to me.'

I'm not fond of children. If Joey had been more active we might have had the one but sometimes I think the maternal bone is lacking from me. I don't mind if they're quiet or so tired they climb up and fall asleep on you. For hugging there's nothing better but mostly they get in the way. I'd not say no to a child you could keep in a drawer and take out for company.

Gretta Ollack was more kindly disposed to them. She'd been a teacher and I suppose the Germans love their children too. The meal ended with Jamie in my lap and me singing him a lullaby.

'It's a Bulgarian folk song,' I said after I'd finished but it was really 'A-Tisket-A-Tasket' with gibberish lyrics.

The Oates were appalled but admiring.

'He'll sleep safe through till morning,' I said handing him back.

They muttered their thanks.

They declined Mrs M.'s offer of an evening in the conservatoiree. They had a drinks do in Chale. I was sorry to see them go. They'd been the first to speak at any length with Gretta Ollack.

'Did you say you came from Poole?' I asked following them out into the hall.

'Yes, do you know it?'

'Sadly, no. I imagine it's quite a quiet place.'

'Quite the contrary. Leslie here is in the ARP and is out most nights. I don't like being left alone but I've since taken up appliqué. With Leslie away I've more elbow room.'

'It'll have a naval base, I daresay.'

Leslie snapped again. 'Excuse me, but why do you want to know?'

'I merely ask out of curiosity.'

'Then don't!'

'Leslie! He's still upset about that fan. We don't have to give it to them.'

'May I direct you, Miss Ollack, to that poster not four and a half inches from your left shoulder, "Careless Talk Costs Lives".'

I grew grand in a moment.

'I hardly think that such trivial detail as has featured in our conversation this evening is in any way likely to boost the German war effort. Do you?'

'It's from such trivial details that a larger picture may be drawn,' said Leslie. He was so pompous. Surveyors are. He was looking at me strange. I looked at him back.

'What was that song you were singing?'

'A Bulgarian folk song.'

'Bulgarian?'

'Well, that's all right then, isn't it, Leslie? Bulgaria's on our side. Or is it Nigeria?'

*

I went back to the table and did my best to eat Mrs McLelland's milk jelly – not an easy dish to damage but she managed. I left it half eaten by pretending I was eager to relax with a sherry in the conservatoiree.

Mrs Gobowen of Sea Idyll was already there.

Now I'm thin with a waist to envy. I look with compassion on the fat and make no criticism but Mrs Gobowen had a figure for which war rations could only be a blessing.

'Forgive my size and my not getting up, Miss Ollack. It's grief has made me big. Aged seventeen they called me the Whippet but I lost my husband early on. He fell off a ladder decorating and I just ballooned overnight. Misery has a way of meddling with the body's proportions. I doubt you know that, Miss Ollack. You're on the bony side. You can only have known joy.'

'I have been fortunate, yes,' I said. I spoke as Gretta. Mabel might have had a different answer.

'Not that it's a golden rule. Take our hostess,' she said as Mrs M. came in with her tray. 'Daisy's had her fair share of trouble. By rights, she should be as big as me. Her husband died the same week as mine. She still hasn't had that back bedroom done and it's, what, twenty years now?'

'I keep it like that as a mausoleum you know an emolument to his memory. I think remembering them is the least you can do for the decreased,' said Mrs M. as she added Jif lemon juice to the sherry.

'Both men left us with young sons and only our skills as landladies to keep us from hunger and privation so now you know why I'm the size I am.'

'It's hard work keeps me trim,' said Mrs M. patting her stomach with her tray, 'that, and not eating.'

Mrs Gobowen was alive to an insult in her words hidden so deeply that no one else would have known it was there.

'I work hard, Daisy McLelland, and don't you say otherwise!'

'And yet,' I said, 'it must be a slim time for you both with the island closed.'

'It's always a slim time. I've people billeted on me from Ventnor. It's still a struggle.'

Mrs M. doled out the sherry. It was the colour of coffee and smelled like a thing you rub on your chest come winter. I sipped at it for politeness's sake. I didn't comment on it being served in tumblers. A woman without wallpaper couldn't be expected to run to schooners.

Somehow the talk turned to Young Jamie to children in general and from there to how both of them were mothers.

'I have a son in Africa,' said Mrs M. so proudly that she might have put him there herself. She showed me his photograph. I saw a stick in uniform. I said he seemed a nice lad.

'I've got a son in Africa,' said Mrs Gobowen not to be outdone, 'but in another part.'

I wondered if Africa wasn't in danger of being over-crowded but confined myself to remarking they probably had good weather there.

Mrs Gobowen also had a photograph. It was in her locket. I was made to lean over and look at it. The picture was small and light in the black conservatoiree was at a premium. I could see only a grey blob. I said with utter frankness her son was a perfect likeness.

'Of course,' I said thinking it was about time for Gretta to shine, 'I am unmarried but as a teacher of young girls . . .'

'Excuse me,' said Mrs Gobowen, 'but I think you're lying.'

My heart I admit skipped more than just a beat.

'Anna!' said Mrs M. clutching her tray for shame.

'In a moment Daisy. I'm sorry if you find my manner blunt. That's how I am. Take it or leave it. You're not telling us the truth. Daisy and me have talked on this . . .'

'We have not talked, Anna! I was just worried and I told you but I didn't think you were going to blurt it out to her face. Oh, Miss Ollack, pray forgive, I . . .' She covered her head with the tray.

I was most put out and not a little frightened.

'I don't think you're who you say you are. You've been lying to us.'

I was flustered and took refuge in hurt dignity.

'What do you mean, Mrs Gobowen? I am who I am. Mrs McLelland has my card and ration book to prove it. You say your manner's blunt and make no apology for it. I'd appreciate it if you were blunter and said exactly what you mean.'

'I'm sure Anna is only trying . . .' Mrs M. fluttered madly but Mrs Gobowen stilled her with a look.

'Sit down, Daisy. I'll deal with this. You should have asked her when she came. We're landladies, Miss Ollack.' She said my name as if it were a bad taste in her mouth. 'Landladies have a nose. We invite people into our homes. In peacetime we need to sniff out the shifty guest who leaves without paying and in wartime we also play our part. There is something you're not telling us and it's this!'

She grabbed my wrist with a cold rough hand. She held it so tight and high it was inches from my face.

'Explain that, Miss Ollack!'

She had noticed – as I had not – the thin puckered ring of flesh on the third finger of my left hand.

She let go of my wrist and sat back in her chair, the white frame of the conservatoiree behind her like a web with her the spider and me the fly but I wasn't to be caught just yet.

'There you pick out my secret sorrow, Mrs Gobowen. I had a husband as you've rightly guessed. I lost him under the wheels of a tram in Macclesfield. An Italian gentleman by the name of Presto, a magician, a *conjurioso serioso*. The ring is buried with him.'

'Oh isn't that lovely,' sighed Mrs M. touched and relieved but Mrs Gobowen was none too pleased.

'So why are you called Ollack? Why not Mrs Presto as any decent widow would call herself?'

Lies are lovely the way they tumble silkily out.

'Presto was his Christian name. That said, I have indeed returned to my maiden name. In these sad and destructive times people here don't take too fondly to a woman called Mrs Mussolini. Oh, no relation to Benito Il Duce Mussolini. In Italy it's as common a name as Gobowen. All sorts get called it. From the high of the land to the scum of the earth. I hope you appreciate my honesty. I should have been more truthful from the start. I am so sorry, Mrs McLelland . . . Daisy.'

At this, unbidden but to great effect, a tear fell down my cheek a talent of which I'd not been aware. Mrs M. quite melted. Mrs Gobowen looked puzzled.

I was doing well. I was a figure of suspicion. I had been discussed. Mention had been made of my ringless finger and no doubt behind my back the hints of foreign travel the red velvet parcel and the noises I made in my room. Over in Chale at a drinks do, Leslie and Naomi would be telling Lenny of a strange woman with an unhealthy interest in Poole.

'So when did this husband of yours die?'

'Not long since but I've always fended for myself.'

'And before Ryde where else did you teach, Miss Ollack, if I can continue to appellate you thus?'

Mrs M. had once read a book on being a hostess. It would have been in big print with pictures. In her head she was leafing through a barely remembered chapter on How To Draw Out Your Guest. If Mrs Gobowen was reading anything with her mind's eye it was How To Spot A Spy. I decided to fly my flag a little higher.

'I've been teaching in Germany.'

More bombs dropped on the Isle of Wight than I was ever to see. None were dropped as elegantly as I dropped the word 'Germany' in that dreary conservatoiree.

'Germany!' said Mrs Gobowen at last. She coughed up

the word like it was a threepenny bit I'd made her swallow. Dazed she'd not fully recovered from my machine-gunning her with Mussolini.

'Yes, Germany. Fascinating country. It's been over a year since I left. I came here the moment war broke out. I wanted', I said slowly dangling each word before them, 'to be where I could be of most use.'

Of most use to who? Neither woman asked. Neither woman dared.

Mrs M. covered her confusion by pouring out more sherry into Mrs Gobowen's tumbler. She missed. It dribbled over Mrs Gobowen's fingers and the woman licked it off them as if this was how she normally took her sherry.

'I do miss Germany so. The people have such lovely manners. The children are very well bred. The child is highly regarded in Germany.'

'They bomb and kill them here,' Mrs Gobowen said her mouth a straight lipless line.

'I taught in a convent. The self-same convent, in fact, where I myself was educated when young.'

'Are you saying you're German?' Mrs Gobowen's hands would have been two clenched fists if one of them hadn't been clutching her sherry tumbler. Mrs M. in the corner was nervously adding to her tray's collection of scratches. I gave one of those silvery laughs Gracie would give me whenever I mentioned the rent, the kind that rises and falls and bubbles up through your words.

'No, no, dear me, no. Anna! Daisy! Ha! Ha! I'm British through and through. But let's put an end to this, um? It's such a pleasant evening and your conservatoiree, Daisy, is a bold asset, not the least bit shabby and depressing. I do so wish I were like you two with your little businesses. I envy you. I even think that in a former life I may well have been a landlady.'

*

I took a polite leave. Neither was sad to see me go. I'd given them much to discuss.

I went for a walk by the sea as was my habit most evenings. I thought then of my dog. I should have taken him with me. He was ever a dog to love larks.

I went down to the bay and up past the redoubt. The soldiers were on guard with guns and two searchlights. As I passed them they said hello as if we were on the same side.

The cliff path's called the Tennyson Way. I doubt he'd have recognised it fringed as it was with barbed wire. The sun was low in the sky. The west was stained red. It could have been Ventnor bombed again.

I walked a fair mile. I was in heels but the ground was firm to the foot. I sat awhile looking at the sea hearing it slap against the rocks. The inside of my head was as smooth as a mirror with just a dull pulse now and then to remind me I was living.

Gracie would have returned from Ryde by now. I'd not left her a key. She'd have to break a window. She'd see then my maps my codes my swastika and Hitler's business in the bathroom. She'd have called the police who were already looking for me. The army would be circling the house. The whole of Sandown would be out of doors saying each to the other how they'd never liked me and had always suspected something. The grocer would remember seeing me get on a bus in a hat and looking evil. They'd all look towards Ventnor ablaze with bombs and they'd blame it on me.

Let them.

I was happy.

I was no politician. I'd had no say in World Events nor had I wanted one. I was a woman best left alone.

People like the Ballantynes see war as a chance to be noble and people like Joey get the chance to be brave. Neither had been as noble or as brave as me.

It was me who stood alone not Britain but me.

Mrs McLelland and Mrs Gobowen led dingy lives. War made them feel important. The Government said 'Send Us Your Sons'. They sent them. Newspapers and the wireless told them what to think. Words I'd never heard before like 'pluck' and 'grit' were in everybody's mouth. Such words held no taste for me.

In the end History would beat me. There are worse things can happen to a person.

I thought my own thoughts. I didn't sulk all quiet in the Villa Judapah. I became a spy and loved my enemies. I went against the tide. I did the unexpected thing. I was like the sea coming back to Cheamish.

The sky blackened and the moon was a blind cat's eye. A German plane came from the west trailing long scarves of thick smoke and fire. It screeched like a thing in pain as it shot across and somersaulted into the sea. Water rose up in a great feathery tower. Two parachutes white, as snowflakes drifted slowly down and landed silently in the sea. I waved. The two airmen waved back. Then two searchlights hit them full in the face. They swam down the glittering corridors of yellow light onto the stony beach where two soldiers were waiting for them with bayonets.

The front door of the Loch Lomond was on the latch. I slipped in intending to make no more nonsense for the night. I would leave early morning and try my luck in Yarmouth but from the conservatoiree came sounds of Mrs M. and Mrs G. conferring. An additional low mumble and sorry whine – as well as their coats hanging up in the hall – told me that the Oates had returned from their drinks do in Chale.

'I wanted to call the police straight away but Daisy here said no.'

'So we've been up to her room instead.'

'There were maps of Freshwater circled in red.'

'And things in code.'

'And a swastika stuck in the soap.'

'Then from the wardrobe we could hear noises.'

'German noises. "She's a Fifth Columnist," I said to Daisy, "Call the police." '

'A spy in my house the shame of it.'

'Leslie could drive over to Chale and fetch Lenny. He's being married tomorrow but I don't think he'd mind if he knew the nation was in peril.'

'Where is she now, Mrs Gobowen?'

'Out. Making mischief.'

'She's not touched young Jamie, has she. When I think of her holding him and singing foreign words at him! All that Nazi filth and he's not recovered from hearing Welsh, as you all know.'

'Call the police, Mrs McLelland.'

'Yes, do.'

'I can't, Mr Oates, I've no telephone.'

'Oh Leslie! She hasn't got a telephone! That woman could come back any moment with young Jamie sleeping upstairs! Leslie!'

'Nip out the back, Mr Oates. The chemist is in the Home Guards. He'll know what to do. Sh! What was that?'

There's never been a staircase built that didn't creak. I leant over the bannister and called through.

'It is I. I've been down to the sea. They pulled two Germans out of the water. Poor things. They were soaked right through but at least, thank God, they were alive. Good night, all.'

I went upstairs slipped off my clothes and sat on the bed drawing maps of the bay. Downstairs I could hear scurrying and whimpers and Mr Oates coming up to rescue a reluctant Jamie. More doors opened and closed. From the sound of it they were barricading themselves into the dining arena. I heard the table being pushed against the door.

I could have left. I could have walked to Yarmouth found a boat and rowed to the mainland but I didn't fancy carrying my luggage in the dark. I switched off the light and twiddled with the wireless. It's a wonder what it picks up in the night.

Down in the street a Home Guard was hiding in the bushes. Even in poor light it was clear his rifle was made of wood. A woman stood some way off. She wore a headsquare and carried a spade. She was the wife of the chemist. She'd not wanted him to meet danger alone.

It was two in the morning and late for me. I fell asleep the wireless cradled in my arms.

I didn't sleep long. The army crept in soft as velvet. Two soldiers kicked down my door. One held a bayonet to my throat, the other a gun to my temple. The wireless crashed to the floor ruined. I feared for my life. For a moment none of it was funny.

'*Achtung, Fraulein*, or you'll get it in the neck!'

Achtung, Fraulein? At that I had to laugh. They really thought I was German.

I said, 'I hope you're going to pay for that wireless you've broken.'

They stood back and let me get up. They looked at me with such hate I couldn't think what I'd done to deserve it. But then they weren't looking at me, they were looking at Gretta Ollack.

They'd not leave the room so I could dress but they said I could take some clothes with me. I didn't take Gracie's frocks. They're probably there to this day, a tourist attraction. I took the curtains instead. I wrapped them around me like a shawl and descended the stairs flanked by soldiers. It was like a Hollywood scene – the exit of the Queen of Sheba.

Outside a crowd had gathered. They rise early in Freshwater. In the hallway Naomi was hiding behind her husband. He looked sallow but brave and in danger of swallowing his moustache he was sucking it so hard. Young Jamie was between his legs. We shared a happy smile.

Mrs M. was by the door pretending to be invisible with her tray up over her face.

'Don't vorry, Mrs M. I have made a note of your name. Ven this war is over there vill be a settling of scores. Your name is at the top of my list.'

I said it in such a funny voice I am surprised she didn't see the joke. She made some sort of reply but it was muffled by the tray.

Mrs Gobowen was beside her. She looked at me as if I were dirt and she defiant in the face of it. She spat at me. I let it hang there on my cheek. I didn't lower myself by raising a hand to wipe it away. Not that I could. My hands had been tied behind my back. I sailed out to meet the crowd thinking 'Mother would have loved this.'

If I'd told the truth the moment I'd been arrested they might well have let me home but what was there at home? No Joey, only Gracie acting grieved and living off my rations. I should have thought of the dog but I was having too much fun to care. I wanted it to go on.

I was taken on the back of a truck to an army camp and made to stand in my nightie with only the curtains looped about me for warmth.

'Name?' I was asked by a sergeant with more nasal hair than could have been comfortable.

'Gretta P. Ollack.'

'Don't waste time, dear. This ID's forged. Real name please?'

I said the first two German names that came to mind.

'Marlene. Marlene Goebbels.'

Very slowly he wrote this down. He even asked me to spell it.

I was searched by the woman who ran the NAAFI

canteen. They had no one else. She smelled of lard and wasn't keen on touching me at first.

'I do like that nightie,' she said as we began to get on. 'I bet you didn't get it round here.'

'No, I've a little woman in Berlin runs them up special. She kits out all us spies. When the Germans invade she's going to set up shop in Newport. Give her my name. You might get a discount.'

'Would you mind if I asked . . . no, I daren't.'

'Go on.'

'Well, could I have a lock of your hair? It's not for me. It's for my next-door neighbour. She'll not believe me otherwise. I mean, it's not every day you meet a spy.'

'All right,' I said with a bad grace although I was flattered. 'Take it from the back where I'll not miss it.'

She held it up to the light surprised to see that German hair was hair like any other.

'You may as well get dressed. I'm not sure what I'm looking for but I've not seen anything untoward. Those curtains are nice. Do you think, before I go,' she said knocking on the door for a soldier, 'you could say a word or two in German?'

'*Danke schön, mein Führer.* Will that do?'

'Mm,' she said considering, 'it's as I thought. An ugly language. I bet you've been glad of the chance to speak English.'

They weren't quite sure what to do with me. For all the talk of Fifth Columnists it was clear they'd not expected to find any. I was put in a hut with chicken wire over the window and a draught from under the door.

They found a WAAF from somewhere. She came flouncing in.

'I hope you realise,' she said, 'I'm in a right mood. I am. So no funny business. I've had to pass up seeing *Gone*

128

With The Wind for this. Bloody Germans. Oh, I like those curtains.'

She was called Irene. We passed a pleasant evening. I told her what happened in *Gone With The Wind* and she said she was glad she hadn't gone. Life was too short to spend half of it watching twaddle. She said she'd only joined up because of family trouble and she'd not been fond of Twickenham. She gave me a cigarette, my first and only. I smoked it for want of anything better to do.

I asked her if she thought I was a spy. She took a while but said that she thought not. I was too obvious to be a spy speaking bits of German and leaving swastikas about the place.

'I just think you're a loony but being so obvious might be your downfall. The army's full of men. The Obvious is all some of them can see.'

Near midnight Irene left and didn't come back. An officer came along.

'Do you know a Mrs Mabel Daley Bancroft?'

'No.'

'I don't suppose you'd tell me if you did.'

'You suppose right. It's not for me to confirm or deny the names of my fellow Fifth Columnists. I say you don't have a draught excluder for that door?'

Sadly it all came close to being sorted.

Gracie Ballantyne supplied them with my photograph which cleared some of the confusion. Now all concerned knew me for Mabel Bancroft but they still thought I was a spy.

I wasn't glad to return to my old name. Marlene Goebbels wouldn't have suited me for long but part of me even now wishes I'd remained Gretta Ollack. This would have allowed Mabel Bancroft to roam uncaptured, a menace to war-torn Britain, a legend, her face on posters across the kingdom.

Knowing my name they quizzed me again. It was two or three in the morning. I made no fuss. I was too excited to sleep.

The sergeant with the nasal hair wrote down my account as though I was spouting Bible truth which I wasn't. I was saying what I liked. They'd nod and ask for more.

'Were you in regular contact with the enemy?'

'Pretty regular. Every Wednesday a submarine would surface outside Sandown about five-ish. We communicated through flashlight but you can't get a decent conversation going in Morse code.'

Outside the stars faded and the sky grew blue. I said I was Goering's mistress and the Germans would land at Christmas during the King's speech. I broke down. I wept. I was very convincing.

They found me an overall and a pair of wellington boots a size too big. I was to be taken to Newport where a man from MI5 had sailed across to meet me.

I felt that important.

The man from MI5 looked barely eighteen but he had a lovely speaking voice. He had that waxy unformed look men have when they've only just stopped being boys. I couldn't have asked for a cleaner set of nails. They used to say the Intelligence Corps badge was a pansy resting on its laurels but he wasn't in uniform. He wore a blue suit with creases so sharp you could have used them to clip hedges.

'Did you have a pleasant journey?' he asked with a smile. This was by way of being a joke because I'd been driven through the night in a truck strapped in with handcuffs.

'You can take those things off her now, Sergeant, and leave us. I don't think Mrs Bancroft is likely to do any harm to either herself or to me.'

He was young but he had authority. That's what a good voice gives. Look at how the Ballantynes had held my Joey in thrall to them. Half the magic of Gretta Ollack had been because she spoke better than me.

'Do you mind if I smoke?'

'No, smoke away. I don't myself but I always have them at the VJ. I keep them in a box in the lounge. Guests dip in when they like. I don't charge.'

'That's very generous. I'm sure you're an excellent land-lady.'

'Hotelier,' I corrected him.

I was fascinated by his hands. When he talked he moved them through the air so slowly they could have been under water. When he held a thing – a file a pen the cup of tea they brought him but not me – he made them seem all holy, sacred. He handled things so delicately.

'Are we ready to start?'

'I don't see why not.'

'You say Hitler intends to invade on Christmas Day.' He glanced at his notes while giving the impression he knew them by heart. 'We need to see evidence for this if we are to believe you.'

'Believe what you like,' I said. This was after all my philosophy.

'I don't believe you. I don't think you're a spy. If you are, you're a very poor one.'

'I do my best.'

'I can't see what the Germans could possibly gain from you. You hold no position of influence. You don't have access to secret information.'

'I am a small cog, I'll grant you that, but even small cogs play their part,' I answered him quick as flick. He couldn't argue with that.

'Wouldn't you think Hitler would prefer to have his

spies in the Admiralty? The Army? The Air Force? The Cabinet?'

'He has spies in all them.'

'Really? You wouldn't give me any of their names?'

'As if I'd do a thing like that. I'll give you a clue to one of them. You'll not believe me.'

'Try me.'

'He's high up the ladder. His initials are WC and he smokes cigars.'

He laughed at that. He had perfect teeth, no sign of decay. You'd think he'd never had a sweet in his life.

'Isn't he a little too high up the ladder?'

'What better disguise?'

He laughed at that too. We were getting on fine.

'You must admit you have not been a particularly successful spy.'

'I don't suppose I could shake a stick at Mata Hari. I'm small fry. I can't apologise for that. I know I've no power. I know I've no prestige. I've not wanted this war. I've fought against it all along but it's been like battering a brick wall with gloved fists. I've made little impression. At least as a spy even in a small way I've done some damage. I've shown I've got nails. I've made some kind of mark.'

I meant to sound proud but he gave me a look that was near to tender. I could see pity in his face. It's a thing I can't abide.

'Hitler loves us,' I said with passion. I may even have meant it. It changed his expression which is what I wanted. 'When he comes I'll open my arms to him. He'll bring us peace. He doesn't want to fight us, only govern us. Somebody always gets to govern us. Why not him?'

'Why not Mr Churchill.'

'Him? He's a spy.'

He didn't laugh this time. He looked impatient.

'Don't you think we can beat Hitler?'

'You haven't beaten him yet. He's just across the Channel.

Throw a stone and you'd hit him. Or maybe not. He's clever. He'd see the stone coming and duck. Then again, you'd probably miss anyway.'

'You like Hitler?'

'Not especially.'

'And Mussolini?'

'Oh, Benito. I've known him since I was a girl. Uncle Ben I call him.'

'Do you call Stalin Uncle Joe?'

'I don't call him anything. He's a Communist. They're working class and bring their troubles on themselves. I'd not have one stay at the Villa Judapah. Who are you? Have you got a name?'

'My name need not concern you, Mrs Bancroft.'

He opened his briefcase. It was leather, unscratched. You can smell the quality. He took out a buff-coloured file. It had my name printed in red.

'Your Fascist sympathies have been known to us for some time. Your name featured on a list of those to be imprisoned on outbreak of war.'

'My name?'

'You escaped imprisonment as a result of an administrative flaw.'

'Excuse me? Say that again.'

'You escaped being put in prison in 1939 because of an administrative flaw.'

This was news to me of a none too pleasant kind. I was confused.

'Explain yourself!' I demanded.

'You were a member of a Fascist organisation from 1929 until its forced dissolution in 1939.'

'I never was.'

'I'm afraid you can't deny it. Unlike you, I have evidence to support any statement I make.'

He handed a copy of one of the minutes taken at a meeting of the Society of Concerned Britons. It was signed with a scrawl from Miss Bird and countersigned by me. It was something she made me do from time to time to make me feel involved.

'I was only at those meetings to serve tea. I'd hand round a plate of cakes and then go off to choir. You can't make anything of that.'

'I'm afraid I can. I also have here your signature on a membership form and on a pledge of a distinctly Fascist nature. There are also various petitions and letters to leading politicians written by the group and jointly signed by you.'

He showed me a whole wodge of paper. I could say none of it was a lie. It only looked like truth.

'We know a great deal about you, Mrs Bancroft. We even have your school reports. Your birth certificate gives your mother's name as Bernadette Taylor. The surname is false but I suppose you know that. Your father is unknown but there's reason to believe he was Italian. Miss Daley refused to confirm this. Mr and Mrs Daley brought you up as their child until his wife left him.'

'Well, your facts are wrong there. My mother was unknown. I was found. And Mrs Daley didn't leave, she died. I was there. I saw it.'

'My information is correct. It comes from four sources. The former headmistress of the local school, a retired police sergeant who lived in Cheamish at the time and from Mr and Miss Daley.'

'I've never heard such lies! Mother died. She's buried in Cheamish.'

He shook his head.

'These are the details over which I do not wish to linger. Gretta Daley left her husband in 1922. She is now a Mrs Costello. She lives in Sunderland. Let us move on. In 1932 you married Joseph John Bancroft and moved to this island. It was then we lost sight of you. The police sergeant was unable to recall your married name and both Mr and Miss Daley refused to offer this information when interviewed in Holloway and Brixton. No one worried about it at the time and we found out by accident six months ago. Someone was looking up back issues of the *Cheshire Chronicle* and there it was.'

'Just a moment. Brixton? Holloway? Father and Miss Bird in jail. Whatever are they doing there?'

'They were there throughout the month of October last year. They were soon released. The Society of Concerned Britons was a small, low-level organisation. Its activities confined to writing letters and a few jumble sales. It posed no serious threat. Your recent actions might make us reconsider but I doubt it. As for the Daleys, they returned to Cheamish. Mr Daley was very ill. How is he?'

'I don't know.'

'You have had no contact with them?'

'None.'

'If that is true, it will be in their favour.'

'All this is all my eye. It is really. It's a joke, isn't it?'

He smiled as if at a child.

'When we discovered your married name, we did not arrest you. We could have done. Under Defence Regulation 18B you would have been imprisoned without trial as a person likely to endanger the safety of the realm. Instead, we had a watch placed on the Villa Judapah. Your house is perfectly situated. It has a complete view of Sandown Bay. If the Germans were to land on the island they would do well to land there.'

Something clicked.

'The soldiers in the next field?'

'Yes. They speak well of you. You made them laugh. The dog they liked less. When you failed to answer your summons your name was wired to me. I issued an immediate warrant for your arrest by which time you had disappeared to Freshwater. This was a silly thing to do. Under Defence Regulation 18B you would have been sent to prison and released after a matter of weeks. Now much worse awaits you.'

'What can be worse than prison?'

'The Death Penalty, Mrs Bancroft.'

I thought death a bit steep for what was after all just a lark. I refused to take it seriously or let it change my ways. I continued to act the spy and was not one jot repentant. I wanted to see how far I could go.

I suspect there was malice involved. I was being punished for disobedience. Those in power like to have their own way. They're not comfortable otherwise. They say we're at war and we're at war jump to it no arguing.

Well, I didn't jump. I argued. I was not to be bossed about. The life you live must be your own. Besides, I was having fun.

As Gretta Ollack I'd had power. I'd had a laugh. I'd queened it over the likes of Mrs Gobowen. I'd sat in the black conservatory with my secret inside me, as full of it as a cat who'd swallowed a mouse other cats hadn't so much as sniffed at. Soldiers didn't call me Crazy Mabel any more. As a spy I had some respect.

I'd not give any of that up easy. I'd not bow down. I'd not confess and tell the truth until I was on that stand in court and then I'd show them all what fools they were.

Most of all I'd show that lad from MI5 with his lies nice and documented to look like the truth. What did he know of my life? Mother didn't leave Father. She died. She'd not have left him for that would have meant leaving me, a thing she'd never have done. It would have meant she'd not cared. I wouldn't have such a thought in my head. Mother died, and that's the truth as I see it.

They gave me for a solicitor a Mr Ricks of Ryde. A dear and frightened soul he had no more presence than a feather.

I was his first case in eight years. He'd retired in 1932. His nephew had taken over but come the war had flown off with the RAF leaving Uncle back in business.

'He thought my great age made it unlikely I'd steal his practice. It sometimes happens. It did during the last war. Men return from fighting to find their clients have been stolen from them. I should know. It happened to me.'

'But I bet you were cunning in your day, Mr Ricks.'

'In my day, perhaps, yes, perhaps I was.'

'But not any more?'

'No, not any more. I'm sorry. I will do my best for you. I do so hate the thought of women being hanged. If they do hang you, I have to come and watch. I'd rather not.'

'Let's hope it doesn't come to that.'

'But it might, Mrs Bancroft, it might.'

They ferried me across to the mainland to stand trial at Winchester Castle. I quite liked the thought of standing trial in a castle. It put me in mind of Mary Queen of Scots who was also done for treason.

'I hope we do lose this war,' I said to Mr Ricks who was with me. Like Joey he didn't like water and was sucking barley sugars to stave off sickness. 'The Germans will think me quite a heroine. They'll soon let me go free. They might even reward me. They might give me this island for services rendered. What do you think? Queen Mabel! You'd best be nice to me, Mr Ricks. Be loyal. I'll help you out when the time comes.'

'All I want is a quiet life,' he moaned at me clutching the rail.

'A quiet life? When have I wanted anything else?'

*

Mr Ricks thought I was guilty although he was too nice to say so to my face. I wasn't doing much to convince him otherwise. I carried on spouting bits of German and loving Hitler louder than was liked. I was pulling folk's legs so hard I wondered they didn't come off in my hand.

They wanted me to be guilty. They were happy to think me a spy. What with bombs falling and Hitler so close I was helping make the war seem real. I was the enemy within. I promoted a sense of danger. That was my role in war-torn Britain.

It's not the role I'd planned but it's not one without honour.

'Don't you worry, Mr Ricks,' I comforted him. 'Wait until I get on that stand. All this fuss'll be over. I'll tell the whole truth of my doings.'

This is what worried him most.

My barrister was Richard Massey Blair Brown which is more names than any one man deserves – although I could think of other worse names that would suit him better. I'll not write them here. I hold no bitterness towards him, none.

His face had a bored and melted look as if he'd been made of wax and set too close to the fire. His lids drooped as did his lips but in describing him I give him more attention than he ever gave me so I'll move on.

I was promised a meeting with him every other day but I didn't see him until five minutes before my trial began. I hardly call that justice but justice played little part in my case although I'm doing my best to be objective.

I was standing in the cell below the court with Mr Ricks wondering if Blair Brown was going to show up at all. I was wearing red, bright red. I'd made a frock from my velvet curtains and very successful I think it was. It was loose and flowing no pads or straps more a robe. I glowed quite scarlet in the gloom and felt very proud with gloves that nearly matched for redness, sixteen-button gloves, murder to do up alone, an unwilling gift from Mr Ricks.

Down the long corridor came swooping Blair Brown the wings of his black gown outspread and floating on the draught of his speedy walk. I held out my hand to say hello.

'This is Mrs Bancroft,' said Mr Ricks pointing without need.

'Good God! She looks like a tart.'

Foolishly I thought he meant I looked good enough to eat. I'd not expected dirty words from a man of his privileges.

'What's she up for? Treason or soliciting?'

At last I caught on and I gave him short shrift for his insinuations and way of talking as if I wasn't there and didn't matter anyway.

'I thought it was evidence and not appearance that mattered in a court of law.' I thought I had him there but men like him are trained to answer back.

'In your case, madam, neither evidence nor appearance are in your favour. Has she nothing else to wear? Can't you find an overcoat we can throw over her?'

'I'm not a budgie in a cage. I made this dress myself.'

He clicked his tongue. 'Ricks, I don't have the time to waste. I'm here as a favour to you. The least you could have done is made your client look respectable.'

'I'm sorry, sir.'

'You were always weak. It's too late to change her now. At least get those damned gloves off her. A very chilling image she presents. "There she stands, Gentlemen of the Jury, steeped to the elbows in the blood of Our Boys." Get them off her now. Now!'

'Please, Mrs Bancroft, if you could just . . .'

'I'll take them off but I'm holding them in my hand. They cost you too much for them not to be seen.'

'You bought her the gloves, Ricks? Good Lord Jesus!'

'I'm sorry, sir, but she seemed to want them so badly and she had no one else . . .'

'Does she want to hang as badly? I'm coming very close to walking out on the pair of you!'

'Oh sir, no!'

'Well, let's get on with it. She's pleading guilty.'

'But I'm not!'

'Be quiet. She's pleading guilty.'

'But when I get on the stand and I tell them the truth, they'll know I'm not guilty. We'll have a good laugh and then go home.'

'Get on the stand? That's the last thing you'll be doing.'

'I will. I've been banking on that.'

'Bank on the appeal instead. We'll get nowhere today. You will plead guilty. You will not take the stand. We're going to have a quick trial and then put up more of a show with the appeal.'

'I have to speak at my own trial. I do. Don't I, Mr Ricks?'

'Please, Mrs Bancroft, it is for the best. Mr Blair Brown is an expert. He knows what is good for you. Do as he says, please.'

I was in an alien world. What did I know of courts and trials and appeals? It was a game whose rules I'd never know and Blair Brown would never show me.

'I will speak at my own trial, I will.' I spoke with more defiance than I felt.

'Then you are a silly woman and deserve to hang. I refuse to represent you. Good day.'

'No, sir. Oh, Mrs Bancroft, call him back. What are you going to do without him? What are you going to do?'

I didn't know. I wished I was at the Villa Judapah. I wished I was at Loch Lomond. I wished I was Gretta P. Ollack who would have known what to do.

'You can't go into court without him, you can't. You'll hang, Mrs Bancroft, and I'll have to come and watch.'

'I'll do as he says. Call him back.'

There are things in life you must just accept like the weather long queues and men like Blair Brown who know more and have more than you ever will. What could I do but obey?

My dress after all the fuss was something of a disappointment. The courtroom was lustreless and grey what with the blackout pinned to the windows and the lamps low to save on gas. Walls the colour of old snow lightened none of it yet I'm sure my dress might have scooped a bright hollow out of the shadows if I'd not had competition from the judge. His robe was not as red but had white collar and cuffs to set it off a treat. There were two others with him in black with gold chains slung about the shoulders. Blair Brown need not have worried. In such company I could hardly be overdressed. Behind his back I slipped on the gloves confident the only attention they'd receive would be the admiring sort.

I pleaded guilty. There were several counts. I'd conspired with people unknown to impede military operations. I'd made maps likely to be of use to the enemy. I'd made codes and signals. I'd cut a military phone wire forced seaguards clipped a few barbed wires. I'd forged documents and trespassed here there and everywhere. They made interfering with plane traps on Culver Down sound like I'd been building an aerodrome for the whole German Air Force.

Read out in a list I sounded as if I'd been busy and of course technically I was guilty. Drawing maps signalling and cutting telephone wires were capital offences. For these I would hang. It seemed a poor show considering my bad hand at map-drawing and how the only thing I'd ever signalled at had been a seal. As for the telephone I couldn't tell them it had been the dog. They'd have put him on trial with me. He'd have been company I suppose.

Courts are a slow business. People mutter terribly. I don't think you should be called on to speak unless you have a voice that carries and something of interest to say. Gracie Ballantyne had neither.

Yes, she was there, witness for the prosecution. So much for loyalty. She smiled up at me as if to say she'd had no choice. I made a point of looking away and playing with my glove buttons.

She said she had known me for nearly six years. I had increasingly made comments contrary to the National Spirit. She gave a few instances and described returning to the VJ the day I left for Freshwater.

'I didn't return from Ryde until quite late. The door was locked. I had no key. I could hear the dog whining. I was frightened. She'd received a summons the day before. She had seemed not to care but such awful thoughts came into my mind when I called and called and no one answered. Her marriage was breaking up. I thought . . . I thought she'd done something dreadful. I ran for help. There were soldiers in the next field. I called to them. They came with axes and broke down the door. Inside the house was dark. By torchlight I saw the maps, the coded messages, the upturned furniture, the swastikas daubed on the walls, the carpet, the staircase. It sickened me. I had such a sense of, well, evil, actually.'

She exaggerated. I can't blame her for that. Given a stage and a tale to tell I'd have done likewise only better. She then fell to doing her Celia Johnson impression choking back tears and being frightfully brave about everything. She said I was a lovely woman. She thought of me as a friend but that I had lost my way, intellectually speaking. This from a woman who couldn't read *Woman's Weekly* without moving her lips.

The rest of the evidence was in depositions. There was no end to them. There was one from the butcher the grocer my hairdresser Alicia one each from the Oateses (none from Young Jamie) Mrs Gobowen and Mrs McLelland (barely literate the pair of them) numerous soldiers with whom I'd had dealings and one from the lad in MI5. His deposition couldn't be read out but it was waved before the jury as if the very fact he'd written it was sorely against me.

Everyone was having their say but me. I sat in the dock happy as a spider caught in her own web.

Blair Brown said he'd call only one witness, Joey. He was called to describe my character and a poor job he made of it. He said I was a good wife but a better landlady. He told them I had no more sense of right and wrong than a spoon knows the taste of soup. I'd come from a troubled family of muddled parentage and wrong ideas but I'd seemed to become normal on marrying him. He pleaded for my life but the judge told him to keep to the point.

I thought a husband couldn't testify against his wife and I asked Mr Ricks if this was so.

'But he's testifying in your defence!'

I'd never have known.

He shouldn't have spoken at all. Things pass between a man and wife which are as sacred as they are secret. He called what he did love. I call it treason. I didn't forgive for a long while and not once had he come to visit me. Burning buildings and strangers under rubble had meant more to him.

He sat down next to Gracie. I saw them hold hands. They were allies. I suppose that made me the axis.

Of course I was found guilty.

'Remember, Mrs Bancroft, we have the appeal. Despair not!' Blair Brown said when the verdict was given. He squeezed my hand and made no comment on the fact that it was gloved.

The judge slipped a square of black silk on his head. It hung over his left eye and gave him a tipsy look. He said I was to be taken to a place of execution and hanged by the neck. They're not pleasant words to hear said of yourself. I was angry and frightened but that little black hat I couldn't take seriously. Caught between laughing and crying I gave myself over to both.

5

I wasn't at my appeal. I thought better of it. It would have been no more my show than the trial had been. Let Blair Brown do his business. He was getting paid for it.

'If I don't go,' I asked Mr Ricks, 'will I be missed?'

'Only by me,' he said. He had a wife six years dead and a sister in Aberdeen. I think he'd grown fond of me.

'I do pray they won't hang you, Mrs Bancroft,' he said.

'That's only because you don't want to come and watch.'

I was acting like I didn't care and perhaps I didn't. You can imagine yourself dying but not dead. What help was caring anyway? My fate was in other folk's hands.

Mr Ricks had hands like Joey's, old man's hands white and freckled like the bellies of fresh trout ready for grilling. He held them out to me for comfort's sake but I let them be.

We were sat by a window in need of a good wipe. The light was grey near to silver. I turned my face to it. I was still young and not unlovely but inside of me I wished I could remain for ever Gretta Ollack.

I looked out onto a yard and high stone wall with not a stitch of grass or nature. Behind us a warden shifted her weight from foot to foot to save on bunions.

'They'll not hang me,' I told him with perfect confidence.

*

As ever I was proved right. I didn't hang.

It was all done on a play of words. The trial judge had talked too carelessly of my *intending* to help the enemy. There was no proof the Germans ever saw my little maps and codes. The appeal decided I was a spy but a very poor one. Hanging was too good for me. I was given fifteen years instead.

'Fifteen years will soon pass,' said Mr Ricks but without conviction. He was to see only two of them. A bomb hit him in Newport as he was boarding a bus. All those years living and he'd never learned to drive. Some people they waste their opportunities.

I should have hanged. I see that now. Hanging might have been a kindness. Dead, I'd be famous. Living and left to rot in prison I could be forgotten and my life lack all importance.

I tell you the law's a lie and I've no faith in it. I was handled with more spite than justice. Disobedience not treason was my real crime. I'd stepped out of line and for that forgiveness is hard to come by.

I saw much the same thing happen to my colleague Lord Haw-Haw. American-born he was and Irish-bred with not one bit of Britishness in him. They hanged him for a traitor none the less.

I'm told in the flesh he was quite an ordinary individual. That's how he was described after he'd been caught and his face was seen full on the front of newspapers. I'm not surprised by the description. He'd had his power taken from him. Without power we're all of us quite ordinary.

People cheered him at his trial. They stood bareheaded in the rain outside the gaol the day he died. He had his fans even then.

History keeps quiet about things like this.

It keeps quiet about me.

History's the lies of those who govern. It does the dirt on those who get governed.

Do I sound bitter? I hope not. All that is past. Bitterness

fades and lasts no longer than hot breath on a cold mirror. Whole days fly by and I pay such thoughts no mind.

Prison suited me well enough. I look back and I think Happy Times. It doesn't do to weep and wail.

Prisons are full of misfits. It's no wonder I felt at home. Not that I was of the common run. I was of a kind unique and this was to be my saving grace.

I was a spy, you see, caught and condemned as such. This was all that was known about me but it was enough to make me justly famed in what was a narrow and inward-looking world. Had I entered as murderess or thief the women would have known what I was and how to treat me but a spy to them was odd and exotic, a spy was to be respected and near to being feared.

Laugh and disbelieve it knowing all you do but to them I was a star. I had all the dark glamour and stolen merit true spies can wrap about themselves. I carried myself like a vase full of my own importance. I was Mabel Daley Bancroft Enemy of the People. Beware is what I made them think until I made them think otherwise.

They'd approach me at mealtimes as if I were a live bomb in their midst the least wrong word would set off but knowing this I'd smile and grow lovable in a moment.

I'd say, 'Hello. Your hair looks nice. You should plait it more often' or 'Is the meat to your liking? They don't cook it long enough to be right tender.'

Soft greeting words like this come quick as spit to any landlady's mouth but as a warm surprise to those who'd expected a quick '*Sieg Heil*' or 'The Eagle lands tonight'. Gob-smacked and grateful they'd swallow down words sweeter than expected.

In such small ways I was found neither dangerous nor mental but normal and rather nice without so much as a trace of a German accent.

I settled in. I made a life. I was considered something special. By war's end I was made Block Mother. I've fewer complaints than would be supposed. I missed my house, my lovely Judapah. I feared the wreck war would make of it and the ruin of my lovely island. I missed the dog. I missed the sea but less than you'd imagine. The sea's a thing you can hold in your head. The sea in your head's not wild but gently soothing. It laps about you nicely and does what it's told. More folk should have the sea in their heads.

This is an honest account. What lies I tell are there by accident or omission. I will admit there were those of whom I was not fond, who held against me grudges for what I'd done not understanding the fun of it or how and why I'd done it. There were minds for ever closed against me. It was not for me to open them.

My first year I shared with a kleptomaniac who didn't wash and spat at me for no other reason than she had a passion for Anthony Eden. She knitted him Balaclavas with slitty eyes and bobbles bigger than were decent. She sent one off each month. I doubt he ever wore them. She was not a woman for whose company I pined.

I had most problems with the wardens. They lived more in the outside world and felt my crimes more keenly.

One of them was never more than barely civil but she worked nights and never bothered me until one morning she slapped me in the face.

'You'll never be free of the evil you've done,' she yelled and then stormed off leaving me none the wiser.

Her husband had been a POW in Japan someone explained. The winter after the war was bad and he was found under a viaduct in Brixton barefoot and dead of the cold. What was all that to me? I'd had no dealings with Japan and have never been to Brixton before or since.

She took early retirement soon after. She started a bird sanctuary in Hove. It's said her sanity was never of the best but it was a vicious slap she gave me. Some mornings I feel it still.

Joey fought fires until the war ended and visited whenever he could.

Why, he'd say, why?

What for?

Were you bored?

Was it me?

Did you not realise?

Did you not think?

Did you not care?

What possessed you?

Why?

'Oh, Joey,' I'd say, 'give over with your questions! Life's not an exam. I don't know why you come. You're not one bit of comfort to me.'

He came more out of duty than of need. Such visits they upset him. He'd begin all bright chit-chat and then dribble to a close. He'd sit across from me with tears in both eyes and every other visitor looking on. I could never comfort him. There'd be this grille between us. I couldn't even pass him a hankie.

After war's end he came less often. He had a job selling fire appliances based in Swindon but with heavy travelling involved.

He ran into Gracie Ballantyne. She was wheeling paraplegics round Wembley, part of the peace effort. There was some talk of her going to Tibet. Perhaps she was into reincarnation and had dreamed Ayres had come back as a yak. It could only be an improvement.

*

1949 proved lucky for us both. Joey had a heart attack and I petitioned for release on compassionate grounds. Joey had the attack in Timothy White's the chemist so at least there'd been medication to hand.

The following year I was out of prison and Joey out of hospital, both physically well but far from happy. We were living in rooms in Swindon with not even exclusive rights to a bathroom. I couldn't see the sense of this and argued for going home to the island and our lovely Judapah.

Joey wouldn't listen. In Sandown he said I was still remembered and remembered far from kindly.

'Let the world forget us, Mabel. You've done your bit of damage now live quiet and unknown with me. It's what I want. I feel entitled.'

'I'm not having that,' I told him straight. 'We're going back, Joey Bancroft, do you hear?'

He heard, he finally accepted but never understood how in Swindon I was no one but in Sandown I was known. I had spent nine years in prison for being a spy. I couldn't let such a fact as that go to waste.

I think the worst thing is to live an undiscovered life and die a stranger to this world. We all want fame but most settle for less, for the love of family and friends perhaps. Fame's been denied me and I've never done well out of family or friends. I've gone instead for a local notoriety although I thirst for something more.

I've had stones thrown at me in Sandown. I've been refused service in shops off and on ever since. People cross roads rather than share a pavement with me never thinking that in doing so they give me what I most desire.

I daresay it's wonderful to live centre stage and hear applause and know it's all for you but if no one claps then boos and catcalls come as second best and must suffice. I am the heroine of my own life – the hardest thing to be – although my heroism's unsung by all but me. When I meet with ignorance and prejudice I pay no mind. I walk on head high with a smile that's near to bliss.

152

My lovely VJ was near derelict. Peeling and broken the life had left it as the sea had once left Cheamish. Barbed wire grew amok in the garden and blackout blinded the windows the glass smashed by vandals not by bombs.

Still pinned by the door was my *Daily Express* Map of the War. Ten years of dust and sorry daylight had turned it dirty yellow and all its flags had disappeared. I lit our first fire with it. It burned a treat.

We set to and resurrected the place. The VJ loved to be pampered. The holiday business was picking up. Boom years were ahead. People had money and were intent on forgetting the war. We were there to help them.

I say 'we' but fail to mean it. Joey's heart recovered from its attack but it was never in the hotel business again.

I wouldn't let him wait at table. His hands shook bad. His aim with a bottle was no longer true. Too many years holding hose pipes I said after he'd sprayed fizzy white wine over a plumber from Crewe. I let him keep to the garden where he could do less damage. My Joey had a sensitive touch. Plants responded to it.

My Joey? I talk of him as mine but he never was. He'd brought me to this island. He'd done my bidding gentle and willing but come the war and after he never listened to me in the same like manner.

He said I was his wife and he was bound to love me. He'd follow me and live with me but he looked at me sometimes and felt ashamed.

These were his very words. He said them as if loving me was punishment, one he'd not deserved having always lived clean and according to his conscience. He said his war had been real and mine all fantasy like Mother dying on the sofa done only for effect.

I told him not to talk so wet or think so deep. I'd not the time to argue with six breakfasts on hand and lamb on a slow roast. He nodded and went out to his shed saying he'd say no more.

Much else went unsaid between us and what was said

got twisted or ignored. There was no major event or larger quarrel but a sad dwindling down of whatever had kept us going. The light was gone from him and from our marriage and neither had been things for burning bright. My Joey just withdrew. I think it was his judgement on me.

Besides I had other concerns more pressing. With Joey hid from me in the garden my only help was a grey-nailed yob who served at table and a slack-mouthed girl who did the heavier cleaning. Guests we had galore but of a lower class than formerly. The men wore socks in bed and no tie at breakfast. The women muttered how I watered down the vinegar. Neither kept an eye on their kids who were charged half price and peed in the fire buckets for a laugh.

It was Gracie Ballantyne who saved us or so she always claimed.

She gallumphed her way back without warning or suit-cases and not a word as to where she'd been in the interval except to say the trains in Tibet were simply *affreux* – a thing she could have read in a guidebook and probably had.

'Mabel, sweetie, *je retourne.*'

She stood in the hallway with arms outstretched as if the world and me should stop and shout yippee just at the sight of her.

'Oh,' I said. 'It's you.'

'Who else?'

She was wearing the coat she'd worn at my trial and her hair was blacker than ever.

'Gracie Ballantyne,' I said, 'there's no shame in going grey.'

She pretended not to follow but up close you could see the blue tide mark round her scalp and her skin was none too peachy either. Later I guessed the reason why.

We could think of nothing more to say so she gave a

laugh like a pianist playing a scale and the very sound of it brought back the spirit of the old VJ. She knew it too and I didn't thank her for saying how dreadfully the place had changed and asking me if flock wallpaper was really the best of innovations.

'Still, Mabel, at least it has a pattern of pagodas. One half expected swastikas.'

She said not a word about the ketchup bottles guests demanded on their tables or the bare-bummed six-year-old trailing sand over the good new carpet.

'We've broadened our clientele,' I said in explanation. 'Have you come back to pay your bill?'

She bit her lip instead of answering and looked over at Joey who'd come in from the lawn with muddy boots.

'She's here for good,' he said. 'I invited her.'

It had been the first time that week he'd spoken to me direct. He said so little to me now that when he did I had to listen.

'Oh, Mabel, what joy! It will be like old times. I could hug you.'

I wouldn't let her so she hugged Joey instead. He was looking at her like a mad cat looks at the moon and I was pretending it was all nothing to me but if she was staying I said she'd have to pull her weight.

'Absolutely! I shall work like a drayhorse, Mabel sweet. I am honestly truly grateful. Ayres and I were so happy here. Oh, what a paradise it seemed. Here I shall always feel him close to me. Do you think such thoughts frightfully morbid? Little girl! Don't trail sand into the hotel. Pick up every grain of sand and deposit it outside. *Immédiatement, s'il vous plaît!* And, Mabel, flowers? This hallway needs flowers, masses of them, so welcoming. Joey, fetch some from the garden. You know the kind I like. And, Mabel, those ketchup bottles. Must they be quite so visible? You used to have such darling sauce boats. Shall we have a sherry to celebrate? Or a gin? Do you have gin? I've developed such a passion for it.'

I pointed out that it was not yet ten in the morning.

'Not yet ten? Never mind. I can wait. It was simply a gesture to mark a new beginning. We will be having wine with our lunch, won't we?'

I made her a receptionist but within a year she'd made herself a badge saying 'Manageress'. I governed my tongue. I could see her value to me. She cheered up Joey and had more authority with the staff. She had me sack Grey Nails and Slack Mouth and take on girls who'd been to Grammar. They thought her smart copied her way of walking and the colour of her lipstick.

Guests liked her too. It made them think they'd gone up in the world to be served by someone of a higher class.

Gracie Ballantyne slunk across the dining room in ever expensive black and held court most evenings in the lounge. Joey made his garden a hymn to her. I stayed in the kitchen the true place of power with my larder alphabetically arranged and the pan handles pointing east – to Germany I told Gracie but in truth a homage to Miss Bird who died in 1954 leaving me a villa in Cheamish which stands empty to this day. I bought olive oil from Boots in tiny bottles and moved towards Italian food – another homage to Miss Bird you see I have some human feeling. It's less fiddly than French and attracted a younger crowd more smart more knowing more foolish with their money.

We took on extra staff. We prospered. We had a write-up in the *Sunday Times* and Eamonn Andrews once stopped the night. I still have the sheet he slept in.

Guests praised us for our tasteful ways and called the VJ very heaven. Late nights they'd ask me one or two about my war and I'd grow fond and gigglish as I told them but Gracie and Joey would always leave before I went too far.

He slept alone. He had a troubled lung. She had more to do with him than me.

She tried not to guess how much I hated her. Some nights we'd stay up talking and almost became friends. Without Ayres I considered her more bearable but I noticed how she walked less steadily with each year and her breath was far from fresh. I kept the keys to the bar. She came back from town with bags that clinked.

I remember one winter we were up late our chat was idle and low. She'd had Ayres's photo made into a cameo and now wore his foolish face as a brooch. Life she said without him was without adventure but she hoped one day to write her memoirs.

'Memoirs?' I said. 'What have you to remember?'

'I have lived, I think, in interesting times.'

'The only person you know of historical note is me. I'm the one who should be writing their memoirs. I've a tale that needs must be told. I could make it sound like *Gone With The Wind* with me as Scarlett O'Hara. She was a woman who stood her ground in time of war and wasn't much liked.'

'I wouldn't trust you to tell such a tale.' She said it almost bluntly.

'And why not?'

'You see the world too crudely and without compassion, Mabel, you always have.'

'These are heavy words,' I said. 'Back them up with evidence.'

'A month ago I met Mrs Gobowen. Accidentally. We didn't plan to meet.'

'Oh yes,' I said.

'You had led me to expect a larger woman, someone crude and aggressive. I didn't find her so. I thought her quite dainty, rather refined. She was with her son.'

I remembered the grey blob in her locket.

'He was also rather quiet, rather gentle, although he had a good war and won a medal for something, he was too modest to say. He held my bags as we talked. They told me that Mrs McLelland . . . Daisy?'

'Yes, Daisy McLelland.'

'That Mrs McLelland died last April, a suicide, poor woman.'

At this I was surprised. I'd never have credited Daisy McLelland with either the imagination or the nerve.

'I suppose her business was bad?'

'That, I can't say. I don't think so. Freshwater seems so madly popular these days. No, she lost a son. He never came back. Mrs Gobowen said she simply gave up hope. People do, she said, and Mrs McLelland was always delicate.'

I wondered about her tin tray and if it had been buried with her. Gracie didn't know.

'They can't blame me for Daisy McLelland's death?'

'No, I don't believe so. How can they?'

'Did they mention me at all?'

'Of course.'

'Still bitter, is she?' Mrs Gobowen had begun a petition against me when I'd returned to the island.

'I defended you. I told her you had given me a home, a job, a reason to go on.'

'That was Joey's doing, not mine.'

'I know, but I told her it was you. It seemed more loyal. I thought Mrs Gobowen a very decent person. I don't think you see people the way they are. I think you see us all as enemies. You caricature us. It's a form, I think, of revenge. I don't mind. I never have. It is how you are, Mabel, but don't commit yourself to paper. People who read it – if any there are – will read into it a different truth than you intend. They will see a silly woman who hates the world and who embarrassed herself for a day and a night in a b&b in Freshwater.'

'And paid for it with ten years in prison.'

'Precisely. What you did was silly and wrong. I would have thought the years would have made you realise this.'

'If the Germans had won, I'd be a heroine. I'd be Dame Mabel with this island at my feet.'

We might have said more but Joey came in wearing wellies and pyjamas. It was past midnight but he kept odd hours. His day and ours seldom coincided. Gracie could no longer control him and I wasn't allowed to try.

'I thought I'd cut back that wisteria,' he said to Gracie. I suppose, although he looked neither at her nor me nor anything as could be seen by sane and healthy eyes.

'Now now, Joey dear, it's dark.'

'So?' he said. 'There's a moon.'

Joey died in 1958 just as we were doing well and could afford to put him in a home. He was found in his shed in his bathrobe and no underwear. I was that ashamed.

Gracie died much later in 1966 drunk in charge of a Volkswagen Beetle. I'd told her this would happen but God knows there's little pleasure in always being right. I buried her with Joey and there's a place left for me in time. I'd have buried her with Ayres Ballantyne but his grave had never been found on account of my never having bought him a stone.

I retired in 1977. I sold the VJ to one of the smaller multi-nationals. They put in four-poster beds and serve beefburgers which I think is a contradiction.

I did well out of the sale and holidayed in Italy and in France. I had a taste of the food I'd been copying all my life. I can't say it was up to much. I much prefer my own.

I also spent a month in Sunderland in search of Mrs Gretta Costello. I'm not sure if I ever found her.

*

My trail led to a Wycliff House, a home for the elderly and infirm. I asked at the office if they knew of such a person convinced I'd find her dead.

'Oh, Gretta,' I was told, 'you'll find her in Day Room One.'

I had someone lead me the way and point her out but there was no need for that in the end.

She lay full stretch on the sofa watching *Emmerdale Farm* her feet in some gentleman's lap. He was filing her toenails with an emery board and they hummed the one to the other. Him I didn't know but her I knew full stop with her wraparound green not purple and the auburn fall of her hair dirt grey and whipped into a vicious bun on top of a face more bone than flesh.

I could have approached but thought better of it. I turned and fled fast as I could my new high heels clacking on the polished floors and her imagined laughter loud in my ears.

Outside in the street I could see her still through the doors of a long french window. I leaned against it and fogged it with my hot and panicky breath. I watched her dead-eyed staring at the telly until perhaps she realised and her bony head tilted my way and trapped me with a look like ice but one which quickly melted. We nodded one to the other or so I like to think and then I walked away.

If it was her I'll never know for sure nor want to.

Cry harder she'd once said, cry harder or I'll float away and not come back. Then where will you be?

Well floated off she had and left me stranded. It was a talent she must have had but one she'd not passed on. I could never have floated off. I'd tried it once and failed. I was always tethered to this world and know this only now.

I came back to Sandown and moved into sheltered accommodation. I have a first-floor flat and can just about see the VJ from my bedroom window if I stand very carefully on a chair and lean out.

I have arthritis and I stoop. My hips twinge most mornings and long walks along the chine and the beach are memories to me now.

I never expected to live so long. Life may well be a blessing but a long one feels like a curse.

Still, I have survived.

I go on.

Where else is there to go?

This memoir's the work of my solitude. I've needed something to pass the time. I've left out bits for economy's sake and dealt overlong with others. I've studied events and personalities I wilfully ignored at the time. There's not a war book in Sandown library that hasn't a pencilled note of mine somewhere in its margins.

It amuses me to read of other people's wars. They have the same satisfying shape of struggle and eventual victory. My own life follows a different more dwindling path, its pattern's less than pleasing. My story was cheated of its proper shape. No matter. Its present shape is its very point.

I was called a fantasist as if that were a crime and me alone guilty of it but Churchill I'm convinced was loopy. Benito only ever had three wheels to his trolley and Hitler spent his final days talking to the wall.

Some days I know how Hitler feels.

Talk of Hitler and I never did know what became of the dog. Gracie said it disappeared. Like its namesake its body was never found. I doubt it's hiding in Brazil.

And I'm forgotten which I think is a crime and the very thing I wanted least to happen. Look in any book and you'll not find me, the only person tried and done for treason during World War II, British, a woman and a landlady. I think I deserve a mention. I think I deserve to be explained.

I have changed in some ways. I read the papers most days. I'm ready for death should it come but I'd still like to know what happens next in Russia or Iran. The last few elections I've even been to vote. The Tories send the nicer car but I don't vote for them. I make a pretty pattern on the ballot paper and ask the driver to drop me at the shops.

My neighbours are as old as me. We don't get on. They remember the war and look down on me for what I was and did. For them the war was a great victory but years pass and now they wonder what it was they won. Younger folk don't care and that I think is worse.

I sit by myself on charabanc trips and no one claps when I win at bingo. I go whole days without seeing a soul and on Sundays I go to church. Christ looks down from his cross. He seems compassionate enough but I doubt he cares that much. I go because the priest is nice and says hello to me in the porch. It's the kindest word I hear all week.

I don't think of my lonely life as a judgement. There's folk who've lived better and more wisely but have ended up faring worse.

I stay here because of the sea. I have a view of it from the kitchen although the arcade is in the way. I think now and then of Cheamish and how it would be to go back.

I read in the papers how there's a hole in the sky and both the poles are melting. Things are really hotting up as Ayres Ballantyne would say. In a hundred years' time the sea will rise one hundred feet.

I find that thought attractive. I'd like to see that happen. Sandown would be lost beneath the waves and that would be a pity but I'd go back to Cheamish where once I was a girl. I'd stand as I used to do on Saint Chad's Hill and watch the sea come flooding back rushing over the long grass the heather the mud the houses and the rest. I'd watch it rise and swirl and foam and I would be an island complete in myself with only the water lapping about me for company's sake.

Yes I'd like to see that happen pray God I see that happen.